DARK

CANCER

(June 22 to July 22)

The most changeable of all signs, Cancer functions on feelings alone. Friendships are very important but with such a volatile personality, Cancer can be insecure and moody. Her feelings can be hurt by the slightest thing. Cancer has a hard time letting go and is very tied to mother and home. Cancers are care-givers – to people, plants and animals.

Chloe is devastated by the death of her mother but finds security in a centre for disturbed adolescents. When this safe haven is threatened and Chloe has to make her own way in the world outside, she finds solace in gardening, then happiness when her overgrown garden is transformed overnight by a secret helper. But who is this secret gardener? And is he hiding a deeper, and more dangerous secret?

Whatever your sun sign, you'll want to read Zodiac, the series written in the stars.

ARIES (Mar 21 to Apr 19)	SECRET IDENTITY
TAURUS (Apr 20 to May 21)	BLACK OUT
GEMINI (May 22 to June 21)	MIRROR IMAGE
CANCER (Jun 22 to Jul 22)	DARK SHADOWS
LEO (Jul 23 to Aug 23)	STAGE FRIGHT
VIRGO (Aug 24 to Sep 23)	DESPERATELY YOURS
LIBRA (Sep 24 to Oct 22)	FROZEN IN TIME
SCORPIO (Oct 23 to Nov 21)	DEATH GRIP
SAGITTARIUS (Nov 22 to Dec 21)	STRANGE DESTINY
CAPRICORN (Dec 22 to Jan 19)	DON'T LOOK BACK
AQUARIUS (Jan 20 to Feb 19)	SECOND SIGHT
PISCES (Feb 20 to Mar 20)	SIXTH SENSE

SERIES CREATED BY JAHNNA N. MALCOLM

CANCER

DARK SHADOWS

JAHNNA N. MALCOLM

Lions
An Imprint of HarperCollins*Publishers*

First published in Lions in 1995

Lions is an imprint of CollinsChildren'sBooks,
a Division of HarperCollins*Publishers* Ltd,
77-85 Fulham Palace Road, Hammersmith, London W6 8JB

1 3 5 7 9 8 6 4 2

ISBN: 0 00 675051 6

Printed and bound in Great Britain by
HarperCollins Manufacturing Ltd, Glasgow.

For Zoaunne LeRoy,
Star Guide and Dear Friend

Chapter One

CANCER (June 22 – July 22)
The confusion sown by Neptune's passage through your solar third house comes to an end. Your thoughts will be clearer. But now the tendrils of uncertainty fall inside your house of home. Let go of the past, Cancer. It's time to start anew! Unlock the doors and step out into the world.

The weatherman on television said it was going to be a picture-perfect day, but Chloe Summerlin didn't believe it for a minute. Anxiety had awakened her at three in the morning. Chloe wasn't able to concentrate on a book and the radio would have disturbed her roommate, so she lay in the dark, rehashing all the details of life before her mother's death – and after.

How long did I lie there worrying? A glance at the clock above the double doors leading out of the centre's television room told her it was a little after eight. *Nearly five hours.*

Just let it go, Chloe, she chided herself. *Whatever's coming, you can't do anything to stop it.*

That was one of the first lessons Dr Laird had taught her. It had been a hard lesson, and she was getting better about accepting it. At least now she thought about it before lapsing into full depressive mode.

Most of the other kids in the room were bleary-eyed from staying up the night before. On Friday and Saturday nights, the centre's lights-out policy was loosened a little. Still, a strict schedule was maintained because most of the kids in the Barrett Centre for Counselling and Psychotherapy couldn't survive without it.

I know I wouldn't have been able to three months ago, Chloe thought as she sipped her hot chocolate.

That was when the Virginia Department of Human Services had discovered her sitting in her back yard eating mustard and crisps. It was in the middle of February, half a metre of snow was on the ground, and she had been wearing only her underwear and a T-shirt.

"Chloe, my geranium bloomed this morning," Matt Irvine said from behind her. "Your kelp plant food really worked."

"That's great, Matt," Chloe said, smiling at

the boy who blinked at her from behind the magnifying lenses in his glasses.

"And smell the leaves." Matt held the plant up close to Chloe's face. "They smell like fresh lemons."

"Umm, that's delicious," Chloe said, taking a deep sniff. "Now just remember to remove the dead foliage and you shouldn't have any more problems."

Matt nodded, swaying uncertainly in his leg braces – braces he was still struggling to accept after a car accident that had left him partially paralyzed.

At twelve, Matt was four years younger than Chloe but they had the same fair complexion and slight build. Visitors to the centre often thought them brother and sister.

Chloe's ivory skin had just a sprinkling of freckles across her nose. Her reddish-blonde tresses were gathered into a ribbon at her neck. She wore a long multicoloured muslin skirt, white T-shirt and a necklace strung with beads she'd made herself.

"Chloe! I'm really angry at you!"

Startled, Chloe turned round and saw Lea Madsen, her roommate, approaching at a near run. "Why? What did I do?"

Lea came to a stop, breathing hard. She

looked upset and hurt. Lea was a little taller than Chloe, with a gaunt figure that she called fat. Her brown hair was cut to a little more than a couple of centimetres all over. She'd chopped it off a few weeks before in a fit of anger at herself for eating a candy bar. Lea wore an enormous sweatshirt and sweat pants that hung loosely on her anorexic body. "I can't believe you didn't tell me."

"Tell you what?" Chloe asked.

"That you were leaving the centre."

Chloe put one hand on Lea's bony shoulder. "Lea, I'm not leaving the centre. Where would I go?"

Lea shrugged away from her touch. "Then you tell me why your brother's here."

"My brother!" Chloe's stomach did a flip-flop. "Skip's *here*?" She hadn't seen him since before her mother died.

Lea nodded. "He's in Doc Laird's office this very minute."

The fear that had threatened to consume Chloe since three that morning folded round her like a thick black cloak. *No! I won't be frightened. I won't.* Chloe took a deep calming breath. "You're sure it's Skip?"

Lea shrugged. "He told Doc Laird he was here for his sister and he named you. He said he didn't know you were in here until a few weeks ago."

This isn't happening. Just ignore it.

Chloe threw her shoulders back and started walking – out of the TV room, past her bedroom that she shared with Lea, to her own safe haven – the sun porch. Rows of plants occupied the window boxes and shelves. Sunlight blazed into the room, making the leaves look greener and the flowers more colourful.

"Chloe, did you hear me?" Lea asked, running to keep up with her. "Your brother wants to take care of you."

Chloe took the blue watering can from the work table at the back of the room and filled it from the tap. She worked as calmly as she could. Today was her regular watering day, and many of the plants would be thirsty.

"I know you heard me. You've got to talk about this, Chloe," Lea advised. "Keeping it bottled up does more harm than good."

"The thought of Skip taking care of me is a complete joke," Chloe said, blinking her large brown eyes at Lea. "I was the one who took care of him. And my mother. I cooked their meals, I did their laundry, I cleaned the house. I gave my mother her medicine and I took her to the doctor."

Chloe's watering can was beginning to shake and she gripped the spout with her other hand to steady it.

"It's funny," Lea said, cocking her head to look at Chloe. "But I didn't even know you had a brother."

"As far as I'm concerned, I haven't." Chloe refilled the watering can and tried to continue her chores but the can was shaking so badly she had to set it down. "When my parents divorced, Skip went with my father. He only came back once and that was when my mother got sick." Chloe squeezed her eyes shut. Painful images of her mother wasting away were painted indelibly on the insides of her eyelids.

Chloe opened her eyes. "Please tell him to go away."

Lea sighed impatiently. "I can't do that. You're going to have to talk to Doc."

Chloe nodded and shuffled numbly towards the door. She'd overcome so much in the last three months, but she could suddenly feel herself slipping backwards towards the precipice. *Don't let him do this to you,* a voice screamed inside her. *You're stronger than that.*

"Chloe, I've got a riddle for you," Katie Newton called from the corridor outside the sun porch. She was juggling with three oranges as she spoke.

"I don't have the time right now," Chloe said, trying to move round Katie.

"Sure you do." Katie continued to block the corridor. She was robust and tanned, wearing jeans and a lavender T-shirt. Her chestnut hair was pulled back in a carefree ponytail with a pink band. The whole time Katie talked, she kept her oranges swirling through the air.

Katie was a manic-depressive, always either up or down with very little time spent between. Today she was on an up. "This won't take a second," Katie said with a bright smile.

"OK, but I've got to hurry." Chloe glanced nervously towards the end of the corridor, where the administrative offices were.

"A cowboy rides into town on Friday, stays three days, and leaves on Friday. How does he do it?"

Chloe could barely concentrate on Katie's riddle. "Um, I don't know."

"Oh, come on," Katie said, keeping the oranges dancing in the air. "You've at least got to guess."

"A time machine," Chloe said, with a shrug.

"Nope. Guess again."

"He crossed the International Date Line."

The oranges swooped in bright arcs round

Katie's head. "Good try, but that only gives you one day."

Chloe threw her hands in the air. "I give up."

"You're too easy. His horse's name was Friday." Katie laughed loudly and stepped round Chloe, keeping the oranges spinning. "When you get time later, come and watch me juggle in the rec room. Joey Startz bet me I couldn't juggle two balls and eat an apple at the same time. I can't wait to see the look on his face when I do it. He hates to lose."

Chloe walked down the corridor, making a wide arc round Earl Levitt, the caretaker and groundsman. Because of the house rules, he was required to smoke outside by his gardening shed, but he always reeked of stale tobacco. Earl was in his late thirties and balding, with a round face pitted with acne scars. His nose was huge and red-veined.

"Chloe," he said in his raspy voice, "Laird wants to see you right away. Your brother's here." Earl scratched his cheek with a yellowed finger. "He's a regular comedian. He should visit more often."

"Oh, puh-leeze," Chloe said with a roll of the eyes. She stepped up her pace to get away from Earl and nearly collided with Sara Barnes, who was just venturing out of her room.

Slight, black, and seventeen years old, Sara kept one hand on the wall and walked in tiny, baby steps down the hall. Sara suffered from agoraphobia and had an incredibly difficult time leaving her room. Dr Laird had finally implemented a rule that Sara had to check in with the front desk three times a day. But even the enclosed space of the centre's hallways were too open for her, which is why she kept one hand on the wall.

Without warning, depression slammed into Chloe and froze her in her tracks. She couldn't remember a time when it hadn't been hovering over her shoulder, just waiting for a weak moment. Seeing Sara with her hand dragging along the wall had opened up all the doubts she had about herself.

I can't see my brother now. I'm too weak. I can't go anywhere.

A strong hand closed over Chloe's upper arm and Chloe gasped and looked up.

The handsome profile was unmistakable. So was the rust-coloured Australian stockman's hat. Eric Irons was seventeen and extremely tall – much taller than Chloe. Broad-shouldered and slim-waisted, his thick black hair was cut short on the sides and left long at the back. As usual, he wore cowboy boots, faded jeans and a denim shirt.

From the side, Eric looked like a cover model for a romance novel. But when he turned to look at her that illusion was shattered. Almost three years before, a terrible fire had disfigured the right side of Eric's face. Even after plastic surgery his features from his hairline to his chin looked like grey, melted wax. Most of his eyebrow had been burnt away, and what was left was crooked. The corner of his mouth was turned down in a perpetual grimace, mirrored by the folded eyelid.

But the biggest scars were inside Eric. As a result of his trauma, he hadn't spoken for over two years. Several counsellors had tried to get him to open up but only recently had he begun to say a few words.

"I'm OK," Chloe said to Eric, whose hazel eyes were full of concern. "I just heard some disturbing news, that's all."

Eric, still holding on to her arm, tilted his head to regard her.

"It's my brother," Chloe explained. "He says he's come to get me."

Eric released her arm and stepped back. Chloe couldn't tell if he was happy or sad about the news. Of all of the patients at the centre and in her support group, Eric was the hardest to read. He often seemed cold and angry, like a wall full of hate. But Chloe also knew he had a more gentle side.

Eric was the person who saw to it that little Frannie Merkel got tooth-fairy money when she lost her first tooth the month before. The centre administration had forgotten to make arrangements for the tooth Frannie had left so hopefully beneath her pillow, but Eric had put the money under her pillow and Frannie had been ecstatic about finding the four shiny quarters left by the tooth-fairy.

"Do you want to go?" The words escaped from his mouth in a whisper.

"No."

"Then tell him that."

The silence between them stretched out for nearly a minute. Chloe had been so surprised to hear Eric speak that she didn't know how to respond. Before she could think of anything to say, Eric was gone.

But his words struck home.

Eric's right, Chloe decided as she marched into Dr Laird's office. *I'll just tell him I'm not going.*

Chapter Two

"Hey, sis." Skip stood in front of the doctor's desk, his arms wide open, ready to hug Chloe. "It's good to see you!"

Chloe didn't smile. She didn't talk. She certainly didn't step into his embrace.

He hasn't changed much. Chloe was surprised. In the months since her mother's death, it seemed so many things had changed for her. But Skip looked just like the Skip she remembered.

Her brother was lean and wiry, with their father's short, curly brown hair. His complexion was darker than hers, partly from exposure to the sun. Arched eyebrows lent a hint of sardonic amusement to his dark green eyes. Most girls, Chloe knew, would think her brother was very cute.

He wore faded Levi 501s, a Western belt with a huge oval buckle, hiking boots, and a San Francisco 49ers maroon-and-gold jersey.

"Hey." Skip dropped his arms slightly. "You

don't seem very happy to see me." The smile never left his face.

Tell him you're not. Explain to him what a louse you think he really is.

"I meant to visit sooner," he continued, "but life has a tendency of getting in the way of things. Right, Doc?" He glanced at Dr Laird for support.

"It can certainly keep us busy," the doctor replied, taking a sip of her ever-present mug of hot coffee. Dr Melissa Laird was in her early forties, old enough to be Chloe's mother, but she came across more as a friend or an older sister. Her red hair was cropped short and she always looked professional, even when she played volleyball with the residents. She wore tan twill trousers, boat shoes, and an olive-green Oxford cloth shirt.

"I've spent the last few months down in Raleigh," Skip explained, "working for Research Triangle Park on some government contracts."

"Doing what?" Chloe's voice was cold and accusing.

Skip was taken aback for only a second. Then his easy charm slid fluidly into place. "Can't tell you, sis," he said, with a conspiratorial wink. "It was a government defence project and I was sworn to secrecy."

"Why aren't you still there?" Over Skip's shoulder, Chloe saw Doc's face. She had raised an eyebrow signalling Chloe to cool her temper.

Skip shrugged. "The contract ended. All of us were let go. I was negotiating for another job with another company when I found out you were here." His voice softened. "I thought you'd be staying with Aunt Vernice. That's what Dad said."

"He was wrong," Chloe said, stiffly.

"Your aunt had three children under the age of eleven at home," Dr Laird explained to Skip. "The possibility of placing Chloe with them was discussed. But after reviewing the situation, all parties involved agreed that, under the circumstances, the best thing was for Chloe to come here."

All parties? They didn't ask me. But Chloe knew that wasn't fair. At the time she was doing her best to imitate a vegetable.

"I didn't know," Skip replied contritely. He looked at Chloe. "Honestly, I didn't."

For a moment, Chloe almost believed him.

"When I found out from Dad that you were here," Skip said, "I tied things up in Raleigh and came out."

"Dad waited three months to tell you?" Chloe said.

Skip looked away and rubbed the back of his neck.

Chloe recognized the trademark sign. *He's lying*.

"Dad and I haven't got on lately," Skip mumbled.

Chloe could believe that. No one had ever got on with their father. But Chloe wasn't about to make it any easier for her brother. She continued to stare at him, her brown eyes dark and hard.

"Maybe now's a good time for us to take a look at the centre," Dr Laird suggested, pushing her chair back from her desk. "Skip, you can see what Chloe's been doing since she's been here."

The familiar smile returned to Skip's face. "Sounds good to me. Have you got a soft drinks machine somewhere? I feel pretty dry."

Dr Laird walked beside Chloe, touching her elbow in a reassuring manner. She let Chloe know she was totally supportive without saying a word.

Skip looked at the selection offered by the vending machine in the break area. "No Jolt?" he asked.

"Afraid not," Dr Laird said.

"I like the caffeine," Skip said as he dropped quarters into the machine and made his selection. "Mountain Dew does OK. Packs more sugar and caffeine than most dark colas." He also got a packet of salsa-flavoured corn chips and a Nestle's Crunch bar. He grinned at Chloe and the therapist. "The three main food groups. You guys want anything?" Both declined.

Chloe tagged along on Dr Laird's guided tour, feeling more and more miserable. The doctor and Skip chatted the whole time. Chloe boycotted their entire conversation, only nodding occasionally. Even Earl the caretaker waved to Skip and told him again what a funny guy he was.

When they reached the sun porch, Dr Laird gestured to the plants round them. "We have Chloe to thank for all of the beautiful flowers and plants. She has singlehandedly turned this room into our own secret garden."

"We call Chloe the girl with the green thumb," Katie Newton said, joining the group on the sun porch. "Chloe can get anything to grow anywhere. But that's part of her nature. Being a Cancer, she's first and foremost a caregiver. They nurture people and plants."

"I'm not really into that astrological stuff," Skip replied with a shrug.

"Oh, you don't have to be," Katie said with a wave of the hand. "I like astrology because sometimes it really can hit the nail on the head –

but mostly because it's a great conversation starter. What sign are you?" Katie squinted one eye shut and studied Skip. "Don't tell me, let me guess..."

Dr Laird's beeper went off and she excused herself, hurrying off to answer her page. Katie and Skip talked while Chloe drifted away from them, touching the plants. They were safe. Plants wouldn't hurt her or abandon her. She could take care of them easily and they would stay.

"An Aries would have been my second guess," Katie said, nodding and smiling at Skip. "But it makes sense, because you seem so confident and outgoing. You probably have a lot of friends."

"Hey, that's me," Skip said, holding his arms open wide. "I was voted Most Congenial in high school. Wasn't I, Chloe?"

Chloe raised her head to look at him. "I don't know. You didn't live with us."

Skip was twenty-one, almost five years older than Chloe. He'd spent most of his teen years with their father.

Skip shoved his hands in the pockets of his jeans and looked at Katie. "Anyway, you're right about astrology being a good conversation starter. And what sign are you?"

Katie rolled her eyes. "I'm a perfect Gemini,

with two very distinct sides to my coin. Well, I must be going. *Ciao*!"

Katie left the room as abruptly as she had arrived.

"She's cool," Skip said, watching Katie make her way down the hall, stopping to chat with anyone who would listen. "Who is she visiting?"

"She's not here visiting anyone," Chloe said in a flat voice. "She lives here."

"She does?" A look of disbelief covered Skip's face as he stared out the doorway. "But she looks so normal."

Chloe snipped the dead leaves and faded flowers from an African violet with more force than was generally needed. "Did you expect Katie to be sitting in a corner, drooling?"

Skip nodded without embarrassment. "Yeah. Pretty much."

Chloe forced herself to take a deep breath. "Tell me what you're doing here."

"I came to get you out of this place," Skip said, looking genuinely surprised. "You don't belong in this nuthouse."

"How do you know that?" Chloe demanded.

"You're my sister. I'd know if you were crazy or not."

Before Chloe could say anything else, Dr

Laird came back into the room.

"Doc," Skip said, "I was just about to tell Chloe about the house."

"What house?" Chloe said.

"Your brother has rented a house nearby. He wants you to live with him. What do you think of the idea, Chloe?" the doctor asked.

"Me, live with Skip?" Chloe gasped. "Away from the centre?" Her chest got suddenly tight. "I don't think I'm ready."

"Sure you are." Skip slapped her on the shoulder. "I'll be with you every step of the way."

Chloe didn't look at her brother. She ducked her head low and spoke in an intense whisper to the doctor. "I'm afraid of going out there. Please. It's too sudden."

"It's time," Dr Laird said in a reassuring voice. "I think you're ready. You've done a lot of good work while you've been in the centre. To turn your back on this opportunity would be a big mistake in my opinion."

"I don't want to go," Chloe said, grabbing the doctor's arm. "There are too many things I've got to finish." She gestured at the plants. "Who'll take care of these?"

"You will." The doctor smiled. "Chloe, you're just going to be living a mile from here.

You'll still be expected to have at least three group sessions with us a week. And that will give you time to take care of the plants."

Chloe wanted to object more, but was afraid to in front of her brother. The centre had been more of a home to her than anywhere else for a long time. She looked pleadingly at Doctor Laird.

"Getting out will be good for you," Dr Laird said. "I promise. You're ready, Chloe, and if you can't see it for yourself, you're just going to have to trust me."

"Sis," Skip said, "there'll be plenty of time to get together with your friends. It's summer time and you won't have to work. With the money from the estate—"

"What money?" Chloe interrupted.

"The money from Mom's insurance and retirement pension," Skip explained. "She left it to provide for you, but I was named as executor. If I'd known that, you'd never have had to set one foot in this place."

It was as if a light bulb had suddenly been turned on. "That's what this is about," Chloe said, putting her hands on her hips. "The money. That's why you came back, isn't it?"

Skip took a step backwards. "Now wait a minute. I came back to try to help you. But the money will help both of us."

Chloe turned to Dr Laird. "Can he do this?"

The doctor's tone was neutral but supportive. "Yes. The DHS administrators took over managing your mother's assets to provide for you, but – looking at the documents Skip has – he's entitled to use them as he sees fit. As long as you're being taken care of."

"That's not fair." Chloe stamped her foot in frustration.

"Chloe," Skip said, "you're acting like I'm some kind of monster."

Chloe wanted to scream, *That's what you are,* but the words caught in her throat.

"It's a really nice house," Skip said, gently. "There's even a garden at the back. A big garden. You can plant anything you want there."

"Are you going to get a job?" Chloe asked, looking sideways at him.

"With the money," Skip replied, "I really don't need to. That will give me more time to take care of you."

Chloe forced herself to face him. "I'm not an invalid. I can take care of myself. But if you're just going to live off Mom's money and lie round the house, I'm not going."

Skip looked at the doctor. "Can she do that?"

"She can get the DHS involved," Dr Laird

said. "Things can become more difficult. It's better if you work this out between you."

Skip rubbed the back of his neck. "Well, if it makes you feel better, I could get a part-time job." He paused. "Deal?"

Chloe nodded reluctantly.

"How soon can you be packed?" Skip asked.

"I think tomorrow would be soon enough," the doctor said. "There's some paperwork that has to be seen to, and Chloe has some things here that will take longer than just a few hours to get together. We need to allow time for the rest of our patients to get used to the idea of Chloe leaving. Some of them get nervous when changes occur. And we'll be making an important announcement this afternoon at group session. I'd like Chloe to be there."

"OK." Skip stuck his hands in his jeans pockets. "What time should I come tomorrow?"

"Ten?" Dr Laird asked, looking at Chloe.

Chloe nodded.

"I'll be here." Skip gave Chloe an awkward hug, then left the room.

Chloe watched him go. *Some guardian. I'm going to be taking care of him all over again. But only until I can find a way out of this mess.*

Chapter Three

"The halfway house is really going to happen?" Katie Newton squealed later that afternoon. She sat in a chair next to Chloe, swaying back and forth, unable to keep still.

Chloe's therapy group had gathered in the big conference room to hear Dr Laird break the good news.

The room was large and, like most rooms in the centre, painted a pale blue. A conference table was shoved against one of the outer walls. The folding chairs were always arranged in a circle for group sessions, and nobody really paid any attention to the one-way mirror at the front of the room any more.

"After all these months, we've been approved for funding," Dr Laird added. Her eyes were twinkling with excitement. "It's hard to believe it's finally going to happen."

"Money's usually the hardest thing to get," Matt Irvine said knowingly. He picked at his trouser legs which were trapped by the braces.

"When my mom went to get my braces from the doctor and we didn't have any money, it took her a long time to get help from the government. I think part of the reason she left was because she got frustrated begging for money for me all the time."

"Dealing with funding is always frustrating," Dr Laird agreed. "But if we care about something or someone, we have to persevere."

Matt nodded.

Looking at Matt's frail body, Chloe felt a little ashamed. For the rest of the morning and at lunchtime, she'd kept to herself, shunning company the way she had done when she first came to the centre. Thinking about living with Skip was frustrating and frightening, but nothing compared to the problems Matt and some of the others faced.

"So where's the house going to be?" Lea asked.

"We haven't picked a spot yet," Dr Laird answered. "Instead of renting, the centre has decided to buy a house. Probably something we can work on ourselves to fix up."

"Can we paint it any way we like?" Joey Startz asked. Joey was boisterous at best, and downright antisocial when his chronic anger got the better of him. A perfectionist and an artist as well, he was constantly doing murals and other art work.

"Within limits," Dr Laird replied with a smile.

Joey's taste for outlandish fantasy scenes was well known. As was his dedication to paint them. While Chloe had been at the centre, Joey had once locked himself in the boys' bathroom with paints and brushes and painted a startling seascape across one wall before a locksmith could open the door.

"However," the doctor warned, "this won't be easy. Already there have been some loud protests from certain community groups."

"Who? What are their names?" Joey demanded. Chloe could see the dark cloud forming on the boy's face.

"You've heard me mention the Citizens' Alliance," the doctor said.

"They're the people who didn't want the centre built here in the first place," Lea said.

"Right." Dr Laird nodded. "And their opinion hasn't changed. They just found out about the funding for the halfway house and already they've started to fight it. A letter was sent to every real estate agent in town warning that anyone who sells to us will be boycotted."

Groans of disappointment filled the room.

"They're all just a bunch of NIMBYS," Joey muttered. "I'd like to take them out and squeeze their tiny pinheads."

"NIMBY?" Katie blinked at Joey. "What's a NIMBY?"

"It means Not In My Back Yard," the doctor explained. "They're the type of people who say they want to help, just so long as they don't have to come in contact with the people they're helping."

"Fine," Katie said, tossing her head from side to side. "Let them keep their little town to themselves. We don't need that kind of grief."

"But I want to get out," Joey complained. "I'm just as good as they are."

"I don't want to go anywhere outside," Sara said. She sat in her usual place in one of the room's corners. "There are just too many people out there. It makes me confused, and I can't think."

"But I'd like to be able to go to the park," Matt said. "And if we got a house, I'd like to have a dog."

"I don't know about anyone else," Kelly Raiford said, "but, personally, I can't wait for the chance to go shopping whenever I feel like it." She twisted a strand of white-blonde hair and popped a pink bubble of gum sharply between her teeth.

Dr Laird nodded but didn't say anything. Everyone at the centre knew Kelly's kleptomaniac habits had put her there.

"I don't like being round people," Lea said. "They look at me in disgust when they see how fat I am."

A chorus of denial followed immediately, which Chloe knew was exactly what Lea wanted.

"At least they look at you," Eric said quietly. "They turn away when they see me."

His words were cold and neutral but Chloe could feel the pain behind them. Everyone turned to stare at him in surprise. Since Eric rarely said more than a mumbled "Yes" or "No", two complete sentences from him was a real shock.

"Eric," Dr Laird said, "is there something you want to talk about?"

As usual Eric was sitting near the back, the Australian stockman's hat shadowing his face. He seemed about to say something, then shook his head.

Dr Laird turned to Chloe and said, "You're being awfully quiet. Usually you have something to contribute."

Chloe sat in a tight knot with her knees pulled

to her chest and her arms wrapped round her legs. She stared at her feet. "What does my opinion matter? I'm being forced to leave."

"What do you mean?" Matt asked.

Quickly, in a shaky voice, Chloe explained how Skip had shown up that morning prepared to take her away from the centre.

"You should be happy he's breaking you out of this place," Kelly Raiford said with another loud pop of gum. "No offence, Doc."

"None taken." Dr Laird sipped her coffee. "You don't seem to be very excited about leaving, Chloe."

"I'm not. I want to stay here. I'm afraid of what might happen when I leave the group."

Within seconds the loose revelry that had started up in the group died away. The other kids leaned forward in their seats. They'd all learned to listen to each other's problems.

"Afraid of what might happen to the group?" Matt asked.

Chloe shook her head. "To me."

"Does your brother Skip frighten you?" Katie asked.

"I'm not worried that he'll hurt me," Chloe tightened her grip round her legs, "if that's what you mean."

Katie nodded.

"But I just can't go back." Chloe's voice caught in her throat. She couldn't talk above a whisper. "My life with Skip was a living hell."

"Can you tell us about it?" Dr Laird asked, setting her mug down and leaning forward.

Chloe looked at all the faces ringing her circle. Even Eric leaned in closer and pushed his hat back with a thumb. *They've been my friends through everything these last few months. They only want to help.*

"Tell us a story," the doctor urged, referring to the story-telling technique she'd taught them. By putting everything into the third person, the members of the group could distance themselves far enough from their problems and memories to deal with them.

Chloe let out a shuddering breath. "Once upon a time, there was a mother, a father, and two little children. When the children were eight and thirteen, their parents divorced after years of fighting. The father took the boy away to live with him while the girl stayed with her mother."

"And how did the girl feel about the father?" Dr Laird asked.

"She didn't like him at all," Chloe said. "The father was big and loud and always angry. He didn't like girls. He would send her to her room and not let her come out."

"What about the boy?"

"He was allowed to go outside and play. Whenever he wanted."

"Were the boy and girl friends?" Dr Laird asked.

Chloe shook her head. "No. The girl resented the boy because he could do anything he wanted. He had friends and she didn't."

"What happened next?"

"When the father and the boy left, the mother and the girl were very happy together. They had very little money, but they took care of each other. There was so much love in their life."

"It sounds wonderful," Katie commented.

"It was," Chloe replied. "Then the mother got sick. The doctors said she was dying, and there was nothing anyone could do. The girl didn't believe the doctors. She thought if she did every thing she could to help her mother, she would get well. But no matter what the daughter did, it wasn't enough."

"That was the illness," the doctor said gently. "Not any fault of the girl's."

Chloe brushed tears from her cheeks. "I know, but the girl didn't know that at the time. Then, when it seemed nothing could be worse, the boy appeared on their doorstep."

"That was worse?" Dr Laird asked.

"Yes. Eight years had gone by, and the boy was no longer a boy. At least, he wasn't supposed to be. He was twenty-one. But he still acted like a boy. A mean, thoughtless boy. The boy scared the girl."

"He reminded her of her father."

Chloe nodded. "Exactly. The boy ruined their life. The boy took money from the mother's purse. Money that should have gone for medicine. He made a mess of the house. He took the car when it was needed to drive the mother to appointments—"

"What did the girl do?" Doc asked.

"What could she do?" Chloe said with a shrug. "Her mother was ill. Any amount of stress only made her more ill. The girl worked twice as hard to keep the peace. She cleaned the house, cooked their meals and never said an unkind word to her brother."

"What did the boy do for the mother?" Lea asked.

Chloe squeezed her eyes shut. "He shortened her life. Sitting there hour after hour, chain-smoking, watching television when the mother needed to sleep."

"It must have been hard for the girl," Dr Laird murmured. "The boy demanding and getting all of the mother's attention."

Chloe's chin began to quiver. "The mother and the daughter had been so close and the boy forced himself between them, never giving them a second to be alone together."

"What happened when the mother died?" the doctor asked.

"The girl had gone to school that day to take her final exams of the semester. The tests took too long. Nearly an entire morning. The girl hadn't wanted to leave her mother, but the brother had insisted she take her exams. He promised to take care of their mother."

Chloe paused, staring off into space.

"And?"

"When the daughter came home, the house was empty. The mother was gone, the brother was gone."

"Where did they go?" Katie asked.

"The girl didn't know. She was frantic. She called the hospitals but couldn't find her mother. It seems she had died and been taken to a funeral home. But the daughter didn't know this."

"Didn't the brother call, or leave her a note?" Matt asked.

"The brother disappeared and was never heard from again." Chloe focused her eyes on Dr Laird. "Until today."

Silence fell upon the room.

The doctor set her mug on the carpet in front of her and ran her hands through her short red hair. "It sounds like the brother couldn't deal with the mother's death."

Chloe nodded. "So he robbed me of the chance to say goodbye to the person who mattered more to me than life itself."

Dr Laird leant forward and clasped Chloe's hands. "But your brother has come back. Maybe now you two can help each other. And maybe you can forgive him – so you can get on with your life."

Chloe pulled her hands away. For the first time since she had entered the centre, she felt certain the doctor was wrong. Dead wrong.

"I'll go live in that house with my brother, because I'm forced to," Chloe said fiercely. "But I will never, *ever* forgive him."

CHAPTER FOUR

Things are looking up in several areas. Trends in your "cosmic cleaning" seem to indicate that you are due for a personal makeover. (A new hairstyle, perhaps?) Something new is entering your life, and you like it at the same time as you fear it. No matter, Cancer – you can handle it.

"There it is!" Skip pointed proudly. "Home."

Seated in the passenger seat of Skip's ancient Toyota, Chloe peered through the smudged window at the block of older two-story Colonial houses. The homes were neat, with well-groomed yards and driveways filled with nearly new cars.

"Which house?" Chloe asked, getting excited. These homes were nice. Like nothing they had ever lived in. *How has Skip managed something as fantastic as this?*

"There." Skip pointed again as they sailed past the half-dozen homes that had been lovingly restored.

The house was hidden behind overgrown forsythia bushes and redbud trees. It was two stories tall, but slumped rather than stood on its lot. A tall hedge separated it from the neighbouring house, with an open field that turned to dense forest only a little beyond.

Once the exterior had been painted a light blue but the paint was so weathered and washed out it was now a dismal grey. The picket fence circling the weed-choked yard was broken down and missing entirely in places.

Skip drove over the hump to the driveway with a harsh bounce that tipped over some of the plants on Chloe's tray. He hit the brakes and announced triumphantly, "Here we are! Home sweet home."

Chloe stared coldly at her brother. "This place is a disaster."

"Hey, it's not all that bad." Skip opened the door and got out of the car. He slipped the cigarette from behind his ear and lit it. "It may be a little run down, but that's why the rent is so cheap."

"They should be paying *you* to stay here," Chloe said, making no move to get out of the car.

"C'mon, sis. I know how much you like old things. You still have Mom's old furniture. And that old silk shawl great-aunt Esther gave you is still around. And what about that china teacup with the crack down the side? I could go on." He gestured at her suitcases in the back of the Toyota.

"I like antiques," Chloe said. "But this place isn't an antique, it's an old, rotten house."

"We can fix it up," Skip said.

"We?"

For a second, the cheery façade Skip was sporting flickered out of existence. "Look, Chloe, you don't have to make this any harder than it already is. Despite whatever you're thinking, I came here to try to help you."

Chloe really wanted to believe him, but her anger surfaced before she could stop it.

"You only came back for the money," she accused.

Skip took another drag on his cigarette and looked away from her. "Think what you want," he said, breathing out smoke. "Just keep in mind I'm the only real family you have."

"Am I supposed to be grateful?" Even as she said it, Chloe felt guilty. That morning, in a private conference with Doctor Laird, she'd discussed the money issue. They'd drawn up a monthly budget together. After estimating her cost of living, the money that Skip would have left over to manage was meagre. If Skip was solely after her money, Dr Laird felt certain he'd give up soon.

The realization made her feel guilty and selfish, the way she'd felt when she was exhausted from taking care of her mother and wished she could just escape.

"Oh, all right." Chloe threw open the car door and got out.

Skip, the smile back on his face, took her tray of plants and offered to carry them into the house. Chloe let him, then reached back into the car for her suitcase and followed him inside.

"This place is a mess," Chloe gasped as they stepped through the front door. "How long have you lived here?"

Screwed-up snack packages and candy bar wrappers, mostly empty aluminum TV dinner trays, cigarette butts, and empty Jolt cola cans and bottles lay scattered all over the front room.

"About a week. But don't worry." Skip placed the tray of plants on the low table at the foot of the stairs. "I'm going to clean everything up. I've just been busy."

"Right," Chloe muttered under her breath.

"There are four bedrooms upstairs," Skip said, picking up an ashtray off the carpet and flicking his cigarette ash in it. "But I've been kind of hanging out down here."

Chloe nodded. The living room was seriously under-stocked on furniture. A nine-inch black-and-white TV with the sound muted sat on a scarred coffee table. A frayed blanket twisted across the sofa, while a couple of gym bags and a backpack held down the love seat. Dirty clothes – at least Chloe assumed they were dirty – were strewn nearby.

"There *is* water and electricity, right?" Chloe asked.

"Sure." Skip nodded enthusiastically. "Stove. Refrigerator. All the comforts of home. It's just that everything's been kind of closed up for awhile."

For the first time, Chloe noticed the floor. She'd expected worn-out carpet or linoleum. Instead, the floor was hardwood and seemed to be reasonably intact. In the corners she caught a gleam of wax.

Kneeling, she took a tissue from her purse and scrubbed at the floor near the wall. The dust came away with some effort, leaving the wood clear below. *With some work, this floor could look magnificent.* Suddenly she was intrigued. Once upon a time someone had taken really good care of the house. *I wonder what happened?*

"Come and see the garden," Skip said, gesturing towards the dining room and the door that lay beyond.

Chloe followed him through the house to the back door. The kitchen was a total disaster. The back door squeaked on rusty hinges when Skip opened it and let Chloe walk ahead of him.

"Oh!" Chloe gasped when she saw the garden. Not with delight, but with painful surprise.

A low stone wall ran round the generous perimeter, bisected by flagstone walkways. Sections of the wall had caved in. A large birdbath supported by three stone seahorses stood by a dilapidated gazebo. The birdbath was filled with reddish-brown water, dead vegetation and moss, and was cracked in three or four places.

An old-fashioned cabbage rose was a mass of tangled brambles. The dogwood tree, which had provided a shaded spot near the gazebo, was in serious need of pruning, and one broken limb hung down to touch the ground. The beds were filled with spikes of thistle overlaying a carpet of overgrown vine.

Still, there were survivors in the morass. The cabbage rose, once it was cleaned up, looked like it would make it. And the dogwood tree would look a lot better after it was pruned. The honeysuckle vines could be cleaned out and spruced up. Through the bindweed, clumps of old peonies refused to totally give in and die out. There were other pockets of iris, bleeding heart, and tiger lilies that cried out for attention.

Skip dropped his cigarette to the ground and crushed it with his boot. "Geez, I'm sorry, Chloe. I looked at the garden, but I guess I never really *looked* at it. This place looks like a battlefield."

"But the war's not over yet," Chloe murmured. Kneeling, she tenderly cleared bindweed away from a clump of red peonies. Once they were freed, the peonies stood up straighter and seemed so much more colourful. "The garden hasn't given up. It's been wounded, but it can heal."

"You really think so?" Skip asked doubtfully.

To her own surprise, Chloe said, "Yes." She stood up. "It'll take a lot of hard work, but it can be done." *The garden needs me. No one else has taken the time for it. But I can do this.* She took a deep breath and smelled the sweet scent of the peonies on her fingers.

"I'm glad you think so." Skip hugged Chloe, but she couldn't respond and he broke it off awkwardly.

Skip stepped away and lit another cigarette. "There's a nursery and garden store not very far away. I think they're open today. Would you like to go?"

"Sure."

"We can pick up some seed and some tools," Skip said. "Of course, we're going to have to empty the car first."

"OK." Chloe turned to go with him.

"Let me do it, sis. I'll just toss everything in the living room and we can sort it out later."

"You don't mind?"

Skip grinned. "If you promise to fix something tonight besides a TV dinner, I'll think I'm getting a bargain."

"I can do that." After he left, Chloe wandered round the garden. She worked on some of the easier problems, pulling out clumps of weeds with her hands. The promise of the garden became more real with every fistful. She was so intent on her work that she didn't see the man staring at her over the neighbouring fence until she was almost under him.

"Aiiieee!" she cried, clapping her hand over her mouth.

"Didn't mean to scare you," the man said. Only the upper half of his head showed over the fence. His skin was a ruddy tan and he wore a cream-coloured fishing hat festooned with colourful lures. His blue eyes regarded her suspiciously. He gripped the top of the fence with huge, gnarled hands and barked, "I thought you saw me."

Despite the pounding of her heart, Chloe said, "I'm OK. I just wasn't paying attention."

The man nodded. "You like gardening?"

"Very much."

"I can tell. Sure is a shame about that one. Used to be a work of art. Yes sir, a real labour of love. It just hasn't been the same since the murder."

"The murder?" Chloe echoed as goose bumps raced up and down her spine.

The man raised his eyebrow. "You didn't know? Figured the renting company might have mentioned that."

"Actually, my brother worked out the agreement. They might have told him." *But he sure didn't tell me!*

"Well, it happened nearly ten years ago. Maybe they just figured that nobody would even remember it."

"What happened?"

"You sure you want to know all this?"

"I'm living here now. I'll probably hear about it sooner or later."

"You're probably right, little lady. What's your name?"

"Chloe Summerlin."

"Colonel Wilson Marquette, retired," the man said, as he stepped on to a bench. He smiled as he reached his hand over the top the fence to shake hers.

"Pleased to meet you, Colonel," Chloe said. "Did the, um, murder take place in the house?" *Oh god, I hope not!*

"No. It was outside in that garden, so you don't have to worry about ghosts rattling chains or moaning while you're trying to sleep."

That's a relief.

"The missus and I were already living next door when it occurred," Colonel Marquette said. "I'd retired from the Marine Corps just a few weeks before. Came straight here from Quantico. Anyway, we had these neighbours. The Clarksons. They were a middle-aged couple like ourselves. Seemed to get along OK. He was in computers, trying to get his own company started up. He was a few years ahead of his time, you know. If she hadn't killed him, he'd have probably been a millionaire by now."

"She?" Chloe repeated hoarsely.

"Yes. One day, Mrs Clarkson raced into that garden and started screaming like she was being killed. Well, I went out to see what was the matter. When I got close to her, she spun round and pointed a shotgun at me. I tried to calm her but she wasn't having any of it. She swore that there were demons living in that garden that were going to take her down to Hell if she didn't get them first. I took a step towards her because I didn't want her to hurt herself, but she fired off a round that clipped branches from that dogwood and turned a birdhouse to splinters."

Chloe felt her throat tighten.

"After that, I backed out of the garden and told the missus to call the police while I kept an eye on Mrs Clarkson. She ranted and raved. Yelled at people and things that weren't even there. I didn't know how many more rounds were in that shotgun. But she went on poking round through those bushes and trees like she was trying to flush something out."

"Nobody knew what she was looking for?"

Marquette shook his head. "No one's ever found anything. Anyway, a few minutes later the police chief arrived with Mr Clarkson, who walked into the back yard and tried to calm his wife. She started screaming at him, saying it was all his fault that their garden was infested with demons. Then, before anyone could stop her, she shot him. Bang!"

Chloe jumped.

"Sorry," the colonel apologized. "Get a little carried away with telling that story."

"Mrs Clarkson shot her husband?" Chloe turned to look at the overgrown garden, seeing the event in her head.

"Yep, she killed him deader than a doorknob. Turned out she didn't have any more shells in the shotgun and the police took her into custody. When they checked her over at the hospital, the sawbones said she had a chemical imbalance that caused her to go off the deep end. But she felt so miserable and guilty she hanged herself in her cell."

"A chemical imbalance?" Chloe echoed, thinking about the kids she'd been in the centre with.

"They said it could have been treated with drugs," Colonel Marquette continued. "Personally, I think there's no cure for insanity at all. Did you notice that big hospital out on the north highway into town?"

Chloe nodded.

"That's a centre for troubled teenagers." The colonel circled his ear with his forefinger. "Crazy kids. I can only imagine what those kids are like. You get these serial murderers, or kids who kill their parents just because they don't agree with them."

Chloe was shocked to hear his words. "I don't think there are murderers at the—"

"I'm a member of the Citizens' Alliance," the colonel said, cutting off her sentence. "We were against that centre when they built it. Now they're talking about putting some kind of halfway house in town so their patients can have free run of the place." The colonel held up his palm. "But I promise you, that's not going to happen."

Chloe nodded, afraid to say anything. She wanted to defend her friends, but she didn't want to alienate Marquette. Besides, she was still reeling from the news that she was living in a house where a murder had been committed.

"Chloe!" Skip called from inside.

"That's my brother," Chloe said, backing towards the house. "We're supposed to be going to the garden store."

"Helmsley's?" the colonel asked.

"I'm not sure. He didn't say and I haven't seen it."

"Probably hers. Right downtown on Main Street. Mrs Helmsley and her husband the judge recently moved up here from Georgia. They're good people to know" Marquette smiled. "She'll get you fixed up all right. And if there's anything I can do to help, just let me know. You've got quite a job ahead of you."

Chloe ran for the back door, forcing herself not to look right or left. If she did, Chloe was certain she'd see one of Mrs Clarkson's demons lurking in the overgrown garden. Then the colonel would discover the truth – that one of the centre's craziest teenagers was his new neighbour!

CHAPTER FIVE

"Chloe, I swear I didn't know about the murder."

Skip pulled his Toyota into a vacant space in the parking lot adjoining the hardware store. Helmsley's garden store was at the south end of Main Street, next door to the Hamilton Recreation Centre. The parking lot was full of small children dressed in white karate kits, accompanied by their mothers and fathers.

"Would you have rented it if you'd known?" Chloe asked, getting out of the car.

"Yes. But it's too late to do anything about it now, even if I wanted to. I've signed a six month lease."

"Maybe the agent could find us another house."

"At this price?" Skip replied. "I doubt it." He finished a Butterfinger candy bar and tossed the wrapper to the ground.

Chloe picked the wrapper up without a word and shoved it into her coat pocket. *I've already got into the habit of picking up after him again.* "You could at least ask."

Skip turned and put his hands on her shoulders, looking her squarely in the eyes. "Do you believe that ghosts and demons live in our garden, Chloe?"

"No. Well...I don't think so." His question had caught her off guard.

"Then what's your worry?" Skip looked both ways and then sauntered across the street.

Chloe jogged to catch up with him. "There's also the little matter of Colonel Marquette and the Citizens' Alliance. What's he going to do when he finds out he's living next to one of the crazies from the centre?"

"He won't find out," Skip said. "Because we won't tell him."

A gang of older teenage boys lounged in front of a comic-book shop on the other side of the street. They were dressed in black jeans and T-shirts with logos of heavy metal bands painted across their fronts. They stared at Skip for a moment, then fixed their attention on Chloe.

"Hey, look." A boy with a "Spawn" T-shirt pointed at Chloe. "It's one of the nuts from the centre."

How could he know? Chloe realized she'd left her ID tag clipped to her purse. The centre's logo was like a neon sign, flashing LOONY.

"Don't touch her," a short pudgy boy jeered. "I hear it's catching. One minute you're fine, and the next you're drooling and peeing your pants."

Chloe could feel her face burning crimson.

"I think you guys are confused," Skip said, stepping close to the boys. "We've just moved into town. My sister applied for a job at the centre. That's all."

The boys looked at each other, not knowing whether to believe Skip or not. He produced his cigarettes and offered them round the gang. Two of them accepted, then took the light he followed with.

"Sorry, dude," the tallest boy said. "Mistakes happen. If your sister's not crazy, we're sorry."

"It's cool," Skip said, ushering Chloe towards Helmsley's. "Catch you later."

"What did you do that for?" Chloe hissed at her brother. "You shouldn't even have talked to those creeps."

"Hey, I was merely fighting fire with charm," Skip said with a shrug. "Did you want a scene right out here on Main Street?"

"No, but I don't like lying. The centre is there to help kids. And those jerks should realize that."

Skip's nostrils flared. "Look, I got them to

stop bugging you. It was the best I could do. Lay off me, will you?"

Chloe chewed her lower lip. She hadn't stood up for her friends when Colonel Marquette had said so many terrible things about them. *You can't expect Skip to do something you weren't willing to do.* "I'm sorry," she murmured, tucking her ID tag into her purse. "It's just that I'm extremely sensitive about the subject."

"Then let's not talk about it any more." They'd reached the garden store and Skip held open the door.

Inside were rows of shelves full of garden supplies. Racks held packages of seeds and bulbs. Coiled hoses and shiny new hoes and rakes in bright greens and oranges hung along the walls.

"Good afternoon, and welcome to Helmsley's," a slim built woman in her forties drawled in a thick Southern accent. "How may we help you?" She was dressed in a crisp blue dress and cream-coloured apron, and stood behind the tall counter near an antique cash register. A notebook covered with flowing script lay open before her.

"Our garden has been declared DOA," Skip said, leaning against the counter. "We're here to try to revive it."

"Do you know what you want?" the woman

asked.

"She does," Skip said, jerking a thumb at Chloe.

"Not really," Chloe said. "I know I want to replant our garden but all I've ever grown are house plants. I'm not sure what I need."

"Has the ground been worked before?" the woman asked.

"It's the old Clarkson place," Skip said with a nod.

The woman's eyebrows rose. "Ah. They used to have quite a nice garde—"

Until the murder, Chloe could almost hear her say.

"Let me get someone to help you." The lady stepped to the door that led to the greenhouse and called, "Robbie!"

"Yes, Mrs Helmsley," a young man's voice answered from the back.

"Come to the front, please." Mrs Helmsley jotted a few quick lines in her notebook. "I've got a speech I have to deliver on Wednesday or I'd help you myself. Robbie Proctor is rather shy, but very knowledgeable about flowers and shrubs."

He is also very good-looking, Chloe thought as the boy appeared at the front desk. Robbie had sun-lightened brown hair and windburnt cheeks, and the whitest smile Chloe had ever seen. He wore a green smock over faded jeans and a pale blue T-shirt.

"What are you looking for?" Robbie asked, in a soft voice.

"Something hard to kill," Chloe replied. "The garden is weed-infested and hasn't been worked in years."

"Well, you'll need to get rid of the weeds first," Robbie said, moving to a corner where the rakes hung. "You know, out with the bad and in with the good."

Chloe smiled and nodded. That's what her therapy group was all about. Getting out the bad thoughts and filling their heads with good thoughts about themselves and the world round them.

Robbie turned to Chloe and smiled shyly. "If you don't mind, I'll just put together a few supplies for preparing your soil."

Chloe waved one hand. "I wouldn't mind at all. In fact I'd be grateful."

She watched as Robbie gathered a rake, weeding tools, gardening gloves and plant food, and set them on the counter. Occasionally he would pause and hold up an item, allowing her to choose between colours. Chloe realized she was smiling. She liked it here. The air was moist and warm, and smelled delicious. Robbie was the complete opposite of the boys she'd met on the street. He seemed gentle and sweet.

"Now for the best part," Robbie announced after he'd stacked the supplies next to Skip. "Let's take a look at the flowers."

If Chloe thought the air smelled good before, just stepping into the glassed-in greenhouse was like being sprayed with a delicious perfume. She closed her eyes and breathed deeply. "Mmm. Heaven."

Robbie nodded. "I've worked here for nearly two years and I still appreciate it."

They strolled between the rows of plants as Robbie filled a cardboard carton with small green containers. His shyness seemed to drop away as he talked about the flowers. "There's larkspur, primroses, and oriental poppies. And let's try some jasmine tobacco." He crushed a leaf in his hand and held it under her nose. "It smells really sweet and takes to the soil easily."

Chloe nodded enthusiastically. "Let's plant lots of those."

She shopped for almost half an hour with Robbie, having a hard time staying within the budget Skip had set for her. When Chloe realized she'd gone over the top, Skip added an extra ten dollars, allowing her to get everything she wanted.

"This was fun," Robbie said, ringing up her purchases. "I almost felt like I was shopping for myself."

After the plants were gathered into six old seedling boxes, Robbie helped carry them to the Toyota. "Don't worry about these plants, Chloe," he said. "They're survivors. If you feed them and water them, they'll take whatever the world has to throw at them."

Chloe nodded.

Skip returned to the car after making a brief trip to the soft drinks machine in front of the community centre. He opened a can of Jolt as he backed out of the parking space. "I think Robbie likes you," he teased.

"Don't," Chloe warned, "unless you want dinner burned."

"Big oops," Skip said. "Consider the matter dropped." He sipped his drink and ahhed with deep-felt satisfaction. "But on a serious note, without any judgement involved, I think he did notice that you were cute."

Chloe pretended not to hear. She gazed lovingly at the plants on the back seat. *Survivors. Well, I'm going to be a survivor, too. In spite of any ghosts or demons who might be lurking in that overgrown garden.*

CHAPTER SIX

Someone has a problem – money? – and you have an unresolved emotional conflict about that money, or that person, or both. It will irritate your delicate skin if you let it. Communication is the key to understanding, and no one is better at soothing a friend's wrinkled brow than you, Cancer.

"How's it going?" Dr Laird asked on Friday.

"It's OK," Chloe answered. This was the second of her weekly sessions with the doctor since she'd left the centre. "Skip and I haven't killed each other."

"You're satisfied with things?"

"I haven't seen the demons in my garden yet, and my neighbour hasn't figured out that I used to be a patient here, so I guess things are OK." Chloe twirled a pencil from the doctor's desk between her fingers like a baton. "Of course, Skip hasn't found a job yet."

"But he's trying?" Dr Laird asked, taking a

sip of her coffee.

Chloe shrugged. "He gets the newspaper every day and circles the help wanted ads."

"Does he go on job interviews?"

Chloe tossed the pencil on to the desk. "He says he does. But I sure haven't seen any results."

"There's nothing wrong with Skip taking his time and finding a good job. Money's not tight, is it?"

"No," Chloe had to admit. "Skip's let me spend a lot more on the garden than I would have expected."

"What about the house?"

"It's fine."

In truth it wasn't fine. The house was a huge mess. Chloe had made a few half-hearted attempts to clean but the job was too overwhelming. The oven in the kitchen was caked with grease. She knew that it would probably take a week of solid scrubbing just to keep it from being a fire hazard. Skip didn't help matters. He never, *ever*, picked up after himself.

"Are you sure?" the doctor asked, clasping her hands together. She tilted her head to peer into Chloe's face.

Chloe avoided the doctor's eyes. She didn't want to admit that she couldn't clean a kitchen.

That sounded really infantile. "I'm sure."

"Is Skip helping?"

"He's been pretty busy with the interviews and the job search," Chloe said, evading the question.

"How does he feel about the situation?" Dr Laird asked.

Chloe made herself smile. "He says my cooking's even better than he remembered." *What cooking? Who could cook in that filthy kitchen?*

"He should appreciate that."

"He does." Chloe felt lousy. This was one of the few times she'd ever lied to Dr Laird.

"Do you feel that Skip needs you?" the doctor asked.

"Yes."

"And how do you feel about that?"

Chloe shrugged. "Scared, I guess."

"You sound like you're dealing with it."

Only because I really think Skip will pack up and leave again. Then I can come back here.

Dr Laird put away her folder. "However things turn out, Chloe, I think this is a positive experience for you. Getting out and meeting people is important. And so is family." Dr Laird pushed herself out of her seat. "Speaking of family, your family here would like you to accompany us on an outing today. If you have time."

"Sure." *Anything to avoid going home.* "Where are we going?"

The doctor grinned. "We're going to Monticello. Since you're so interested in planting a garden in your new back yard, this trip should be right up your alley. Jefferson's gardens are legendary."

An hour later, Chloe and Lea were boarding the small yellow bus that belonged to the centre.

"Katie's hit a slump," Lea whispered as they climbed the narrow metal steps.

"She'll pull out of it," Chloe whispered back.

Katie was already on the bus and had taken the back seat where she sat with her forehead pressed against the window. Despair was etched across her features.

"I hope she does soon," Lea said, slipping into a seat across from Chloe. Lea was clad in two layers of sweat pants that hung on her bony body. But the extra layers couldn't disguise the fact that Lea had lost more weight. Chloe worried about her.

"Sara was having a bad day," Lea continued her report. "She couldn't leave her room. And Joey went berserk last night. He punched a hole in his bedroom wall."

"So who's going on the trip?" Chloe asked, staring out of the window towards the centre's front entrance.

She watched as Matt Irvine hobbled through the double doors and paused to catch his breath. The effort of walking from his room at the back of the building to the front had left him winded. Eric, in his familiar Australian stockman's hat, appeared at Matt's side and guided him towards the school bus.

"I guess it's just you, me, Katie and those two," Lea said as the boys made their way on to the bus. "We're the healthy ones."

"Speak for yourself," Chloe murmured, slumping down in her bus seat. She'd had two sessions with Doctor Laird this week but had been unable to tell her the truth about what was happening at her house.

"What's going on?" Lea asked, pinching her eyebrows together.

"Nothing," Chloe answered.

"Come on, you can tell me."

"I am telling you," Chloe replied. "Nothing is happening. My brother spends the days circling the help wanted ads but never calls anyone."

"Are you sure?" Lea asked, as Matt and Eric slid into the seats in front of the girls. "Maybe he goes to interviews when you're out."

Chloe looked at Lea. "I never leave the house. Skip only goes out to buy junk food and cigarettes."

"What about when you're working in your garden?" Lea asked.

Chloe winced, keeping her eyes squeezed shut. "I'm not working in the garden yet. The plants I bought are still sitting in their cartons. They're probably dead by now."

"But you're the girl with the green thumb!" Matt exclaimed, joining their conversation. "What happened?"

"I bought the flowers – but then I realized it would take an entire summer to clear away the weeds and rotten wood before I could even plant them. I tried to start weeding and after a day I'd only cleared a tiny patch. It was so depressing that I just gave up."

"Give up? You?" Matt cried. "You're a Cancer, you can't give up. It is your star-driven destiny to help living things – whether you like it or not."

Chloe chuckled. "Now you're starting to sound like Katie."

Dr Laird suddenly appeared in the front of the bus. "Hi folks! Ready for our big trip?"

Without waiting for a response, she slid

behind the steering wheel, set her mug on the dashboard and pulled the double bus doors shut. "Next stop, Monticello."

On the ride over, Lea got Chloe to continue telling them about her new life. It was hard for Chloe to find anything good to say about it. "My living room is filled with junk food wrappers, the house is a total wreck and I can't think where to start to clean it. And my garden is infested with ghosts and demons."

"Did she say *ghosts*?" Matt asked.

"Yes," Lea said. "And demons. All of your favourite subjects."

"Cool," Matt said, with a nod. Everyone knew how much he liked horror novels. "So tell us about your demons."

Without meaning to, Chloe suddenly found herself the centre of attention. The story of the murder, the possible ghost and the garden demons occupied everyone's attention, and even brought Katie up from her depression.

"You know," Katie called from the back, "it's possible the garden was built on some kind of sacrificial altar. Or near a gateway to another world. Maybe even a burial ground."

Matt and Lea agreed.

"Maybe you should dig round back there," Matt said. "But if you start turning up any graves, you might want to think about leaving in a hurry."

"Don't worry," Chloe chuckled. "I'll be out of there like a shot."

"As far as demons go," Matt said, "it could be that one of them made Mrs Clarkson fall in love with him. Seduced her and drove her crazy enough to kill her husband."

"Doc, you need to cut back on Matt's horror intake," Lea called to the front.

"Hey," Matt protested, his feathers ruffled, "all I was trying to do was tell Chloe to take care of herself. You know why people get eaten by monsters? Because they don't believe in them until it's too late. One step away from being soup-meat, then – BOOM! – they're believers. And lunch."

"Ew!" Lea and Chloe squealed. "Gross!"

The group spent the rest of the trip discussing their favourite horror movies. It seemed as if only a few minutes had passed when Dr Laird announced from the front of the bus, "Monticello. Dead ahead."

Dr Laird followed a winding road to a parking lot halfway up the hill. She pulled the bus to a stop beside an area marked "Shuttle arrival and departure", and the five passengers eagerly headed for the doors.

"All of you know that Thomas Jefferson authored the Declaration of Independence," Dr Laird said as she gathered the group in front of the waiting shuttle. "But did you also know that he served as Governor of Virginia, Minister to France, and was President George Washington's first Secretary of State?"

"You left out that he was our third President," Matt called from the back of the group. Eric was helping him up the incline on to the shuttle.

"That's some résumé," Lea murmured as the shuttle pulled away from the kerb.

Minutes later they were at the top of the hill and Monticello in all its classical glory spread out before them.

"Oh my god," Chloe cried as they circled round the gardens. "Look at the flowers!"

Throughout the orchards, across vegetable gardens round Monticello, were dozens of flowerbeds at the four corners of the house. They held a profusion of blooms in all shapes and colours. Chloe had never expected to see such breathtaking beauty. Monticello was a living work of art.

"Where should we go first?" Lea asked, as they got off the shuttle. "Inside or out?"

A man in a dark green coat waiting on the front steps of the mansion answered her question. "A guide will take you through the house and then you can explore the gardens on your own. Let's see, Mrs Helmsley will be your guide this afternoon. Here she comes now."

The name caught Chloe's attention at once. *It must be a coincidence.* She turned in the direction the man had gestured, and saw the woman from the garden store approaching.

There was nowhere to hide.

Hurriedly, Chloe dug in her purse and found a pair of black-lensed sunglasses. She slid them on, drawing a curious stare from Eric, though he said nothing.

"Pay attention," Dr Laird told the group, as Mrs Helmsley approached. "Thomas Jefferson was probably one of the greatest men in history."

"Good afternoon," Mrs Helmsley said, flashing a wide smile. "I'm Lena Helmsley and I'll be your—" Her voice caught in her throat as she spied Eric's disfigured face. She wrinkled her nose and took a few steps backwards.

"Is something the matter?" Dr Laird asked.

"What?" Mrs Helmsley looked from Eric to Matt, who hobbled closer so he could hear their tour guide. Then her eyes settled on Chloe and for a moment there was a spark of recognition. "Um, no, actually, I think your group needs a different, um, guide."

"Why is that?" the doctor asked.

Mrs Helmsley turned and whispered very deliberately, "Well, I'm not sure this group is capable of handling the information I have to offer."

"Look, most of my kids are quite smart," Dr Laird said, bristling defensively. "Overachievers, you might say. You don't have to worry about them being able to keep up. I'm sure they could teach you a thing or two about Mr Jefferson."

Mrs Helmsley looked shocked. Chloe didn't know whether it was over the information or Dr Laird's brusque behaviour. "But I thought they were from the ward."

"The centre is *not* a ward," Dr Laird corrected. "Or an asylum. We help troubled kids recover from their problems, so they can leave the centre and lead normal lives."

Mrs Helmsley glanced nervously over her shoulder. "But I've heard about some of their tempers. They can get quite violent."

The doctor let out an exasperated sigh. "This isn't working out. We're quite capable of touring this site by ourselves. So if you'll just step aside, we'd like to get on with our outing."

"That's telling her, Doc!" Matt cheered.

Eric, however, had been deeply stung by Mrs Helmsley's reaction. He didn't lift his head until they had passed through the crowd of tourists admiring the huge pendulum clock in the front hall and entered Jefferson's study.

There they found a Windsor bench, a revolving chair, a revolving-top table and a telescope on the masonry pier in the south window. On the shelves flanking the doorway were two globes, one terrestrial and the other celestial, with countries and constellations marked as they'd been known in Jefferson's time.

"The man was a genius," Eric murmured softly.

"What?" Chloe moved close to hear Eric. "What did you say, Eric?"

He gestured to the inventions that lined the study – Jefferson's four part music stand, the double doors that opened simultaneously, even the first copy machine, which consisted of two pens wired together. "Beautiful."

Chloe nodded. "This was a man who knew how to live life to the fullest."

After touring the kitchens, smokehouse and wine cellar, the last site they visited was the garden and orchard.

Chloe stood with the others beneath the pavilion where Jefferson had liked to sit and read. Eric, who had brought along his camera, kept the shutter clicking constantly.

Twenty-five metres wide and three hundred metres long, the garden occupied the southern slope of the mountain under plenty of sun. A stone wall bisected it.

"Over two hundred and fifty varieties of vegetables and herbs have been grown here," Dr Laird read aloud from the guidebook. "Jefferson experimented with several homeopathic medicines and grew his own herbs for that purpose. He also introduced many flowers and trees to this part of the country, including the Colombian lily that was brought back by the Lewis and Clark expedition, as well as European imports like the tulip and sweet william. Remember, this was no ornamental garden but one that supplied the household with many necessities. But Jefferson felt there should be no separation between the aesthetic beauty of an object and its function."

Jefferson's caring hand was visible everywhere, in the neatly interlacing rows of plants, the careful blending of flowers and herbs to delight all the senses. He seemed to have missed no detail.

Back at the bus, Chloe stared out over the flowering garden one last time. Beside her Eric rewound a roll of film and put his camera away.

He cocked his head to look at her.

"I wish I had the courage to work in my garden," she said in a small voice.

"You do, Chloe," Eric murmured.

She turned to him. "I think, with a lot of effort, it could be beautiful, too. Maybe not as beautiful as Monticello, but lovely enough for me."

CHAPTER SEVEN

Not a good time for making decisions while that changeable Moon is squaring Neptune in the celestial gavotte. Take time to mull it over and your mind will be clearer. Otherwise, you risk repeating mistakes of the past – and as the Bard wrote, "that way madness lies".

"I'm having trouble with my primrose," Chloe told Robbie at Helmsley's garden store on the following day. Inspired by the visit to Monticello, she was determined to rescue her dying flowers.

"It does look bad," Robbie said, inspecting the yellow flower. "Where's it been sitting?"

Chloe was embarrassed to tell him she'd just abandoned the plant and all of the others on her back porch. "It's been outside. In the sun."

"Ah." Robbie nodded. "That's why this primrose looks so wilted and unhappy. It can't take direct sunlight."

"Really?"

"This is a woodland plant. It's not used to the sun's powerful rays. You see, plant leaves burn just like your skin, only this primrose can't put on sunscreen."

Chloe looked in dismay at her poor little flower. "I didn't realize that. I feel terrible."

Up till now, Robbie had kept his eyes focused totally on the plant. He looked up at Chloe, a mild blush colouring his cheeks. "Don't worry, you haven't killed it. You just need to keep it really moist."

Chloe nodded. "Water it a lot."

"And mist it. And when you're ready to plant it, set it in a shady spot."

Chloe thought of the area under her dogwood tree. "I know just the place."

"Good." Robbie looked back at the plant and murmured, "I seem to recall that you bought quite a few flowers. How are they doing?"

Chloe could feel her face heating up. "Some are holding up better than others," she confessed. "But they all probably need to be planted soon."

"Well, each plant requires different care," Robbie advised. "While this primrose is a shade-lover, others require full sun. Be sure and read the labels in each container."

"I will," Chloe declared fervently. "As soon as I get home." At the same time part of her was vowing to hurry home and get to work in her garden, another little voice inside her was saying, *Why did you buy so many plants? You don't know what you're doing. That yard is full of weeds. It'll be weeks before you can put those plants in the ground. Who are you trying to kid??*

"Your house is next to Colonel Marquette's place, isn't it?" Robbie asked, carefully touching one of the leaves of the primrose.

"Yes."

"Have you talked to him about your plants?" Robbie squinted one eye shut and peered up at her. "He may be able to help you."

The farther away I stay from Colonel Marquette, the better, Chloe thought. But she forced a big smile and said, "I'll ask him the next time I see him."

"Remember," Robbie said, as he handed her back the sick plant, "lots of water. No sun."

"Got it." Chloe started to leave, then turned back. "Oh, and thanks, Robbie, for your help."

Robbie's cheeks, which had been a mild pink, blazed red. "Any time," he said, with a stiff wave. "Um, See you!"

She left the store, carrying her wilted primrose. Down the street at the single-story bank on the corner, a clock gave the time and temperature in washed-out digital yellow numbers: 11:04 AM, 98° F.

Her feet were tired and her body ached. All she wanted to do was go home. Still, the vision of Thomas Jefferson's garden remained vivid in her mind. *I might not have his genius, but I should be able to get a few flowers to grow.*

After stopping at the drugstore to buy a soft drink, water the primrose, and borrow the air-conditioning for a brief respite, Chloe started walking again.

"What the—?" Chloe exclaimed upon seeing Skip's Toyota parked next to the grease pit at Kelly's Gas-and-Go service station.

Her brother was leaning against the red soft drinks machine in front of the station, chatting to a guy seated in a lawn chair. The guy was obviously the attendant because his light-blue work clothes were covered with grease stains. Skip talked animatedly, in between sips from a can of Jolt and munches of corn chips from the bag he held.

The service station was old and rundown. Used tyres were stacked in front of the single-bay garage, and crumpled oil cans overflowed from a nearby trash can. A crudely lettered sign in one of the streaked windows read BAGS OF ICE – $1; FEEDER PIGS – MAKE OFFER.

Chloe cupped one hand round her mouth and shouted, "I thought you had a big job interview today."

Skip turned, guilty surprise written all over his face. "Hey, sis," he called. "What are you doing here?"

"I had to talk to Robbie at the garden store," she replied, moving towards her brother. "I thought your day was booked with important meetings."

"It is," Skip said, crumpling his chips bag. "I'm just taking a lunch break."

The guy in the lawn chair stared at Chloe. Lately she had taken to wearing the old straw hat and faded overalls that had belonged her mother. They hung loosely on her, which made Skip say she looked like one of the homeless.

"Have you met Leon?" Skip asked.

"No." *And I don't really want to, thank you very much.*

"He's Earl's cousin," Skip explained. "You know, the caretaker at the centre."

Leon looked as if he was in his mid-twenties. Dirty blond hair hung to his shoulders, framing a sunburnt face that didn't look as if it would ever get tanned. His eyes were a fierce blue beneath the curved peak of his baseball cap. He was short and heavy-set, and grease stains seemed permanently etched into his thick, stubby hands. "I can see the family resemblance," Chloe said.

"Leon, this is my sister, Chloe," Skip said, gesturing to her with his cola can.

"Howdy," Leon said, lifting his baseball cap. "So how do you like living in a haunted house?"

"I didn't know that it was," Chloe replied.

"Sure is." Leon nodded emphatically. "Gave me one of my worst scares when I was in high school. Had a flat tyre near there and had to walk right by it. I swear to this day that I saw old lady Clarkson wandering round back there with that shotgun. Want a Coke?"

"No thanks." Chloe looked at Skip. "Since you're on your *lunch break*, maybe you can give me a ride home."

Skip glanced at his watch and shook his head. "Sorry. I've got to be at an interview in ten minutes."

"Oh, really?" Chloe was hot and sweaty, and feeling very irritated with her brother. "You expect me to believe that?"

Skip crumpled his drink can and threw it at the overflowing trash can. It fell short, joining the other empty cans littering the ground. "I don't expect you to believe anything. But you've still got to walk."

"Oooh!" Chloe was so frustrated she nearly hurled her plant at her brother's back as he sauntered towards his beat-up Toyota.

Half an hour later she arrived home, completely drenched with sweat. Colonel Marquette was at the mailbox when she arrived.

"Hello," Chloe said.

The colonel nodded, but didn't make eye contact. Usually he was more friendly.

"Is anything wrong?" Chloe asked, thinking something might be the matter with his wife, who suffered from asthma.

"I'm trying to be civil," the colonel replied. "I find that difficult when I'm angry."

Chloe took a step backwards. "I don't understand."

The colonel closed his box with a clang. "You lied to me, young lady. I don't like liars."

Chloe shook her head, trying to figure out what the man was talking about.

"I had a long talk with Mrs Helmsley this morning," the colonel said. "At our monthly planning committee for beautification of the town. She told me about seeing you with those other patients from that ward." His eyes were flinty and hard. "I don't like the idea of living next to a loose cannon." He tucked his mail under his arm. "I've already done that."

Executing a perfect about-face, he walked away. "Rest assured that I'll be taking this up with your house agent," he called over his shoulder. "I'm not without influence in this town."

Numb and pushed beyond her limits, Chloe left the mail in the box and walked to the house. Her chest was so tight it was hard to breathe.

She made her way through the living room where old newspapers lay scattered across the furniture and the floor. She didn't even pause to pick up her brother's candy bar wrappers or cigarette butts. Instead she stumbled towards her bedroom. All she wanted to do was hide.

Once inside her room she paused at the window and looked down on her garden. She saw it for what it really was. *A hopeless weedpit.*

She set the primrose on the bedside table. "Sorry, little fella," she told the plant, "you're on your own."

Then she got into bed without removing her shoes and pulled her grandmother's tattered quilt over her head. The anger gave way to the old familiar numbness. Chloe sighed as she retreated to that place of no feelings. She lay on her bed and waited for night to fall.

No sound invaded her space until hours later when glass broke, ringing and strident.

Chloe's eyes popped open and she looked at

the luminous dial of the old-fashioned travel clock she'd found at a flea market the previous summer – 1.12 a.m. She pushed herself out of bed and pulled on one of her mother's old robes. *Is it a burglar? Why aren't there any other noises?*

"Skip?"

"Chloe? You OK?"

"Yes. What was that?" She crept down the narrow stairs, avoiding the three loose steps.

Skip was standing in the middle of the living room. A blanket disarranged on the couch testified that he'd been sleeping there. No lights were on. "Somebody threw a rock through the window."

Chloe saw it in the centre of the hardwood floor. She picked up the rock and found a piece of paper attached to it with rubber bands. "Did you see anyone?"

"A pick-up," Skip replied, hitching up his sweat pants. He lit a cigarette and the orange flame carved hollows in his face. "It was running with its lights out, so I didn't see a licence plate."

Stripping off the rubber bands, Chloe freed the paper and unfolded it.

"What's that?" Skip asked, bringing his lighter closer.

"A note," Chloe said, looking at the neat

block letters printed on the paper:

GET OUT RETARDS! BEFORE SOMETHING BAD HAPPENS TO YOU! WE DON'T NEED YOUR KIND HERE!

"Well." Skip extinguished the lighter. "I guess we know who that was intended for."

Chloe didn't bother to look at her brother. She crumpled the note and dropped it on the floor as she headed back up the stairs.

Her sleep was interrupted once more that night. By a rustling outside her window.

Scritch. Scritch.

She tried to raise her head to listen, but she couldn't. Sleep had made her limbs too heavy to lift.

Scritch. Scritch.

Something was definitely outside her window, but someone else would have to discover what it was. Chloe was just too tired to move.

CHAPTER EIGHT

So much has happened in your life of late that it would be a shame to let depression get you down. This Mercury retrograde period is frustrating, but not insurmountable. The Uranian aspect to your personal life promises a surprise. With that retro Mercury, it may be a surprise turnabout in your thinking!

"Open this door."

Chloe woke up slowly, mired by the malaise she'd been feeling for the past seven days. She glanced at the clock. A quarter to eight. But was it morning or night?

"Either you open up, or I'm breaking the lock," Skip warned.

Chloe ran her hands through her hair and sat up groggily. It didn't matter. Lately she'd taken to sleeping in whatever she fell asleep in anyway. She had on jeans and a T-shirt that she'd worn the day before. Or maybe she'd put them on the day before that. She wasn't sure.

She slowly rolled out of bed and shuffled to the door, turning the key in the lock. Ever since the rock had been thrown through the window and she'd heard those strange sounds coming from outside, Chloe had kept the door locked.

Skip hadn't seemed to care. In fact she guessed he was relieved that he didn't have to talk to her.

"What do you want?" she asked, through the closed door.

"To talk about the garden. Are you dressed?"

"Yes."

Without another word, Skip flung open the door. A cigarette dangled from his lips and Chloe backed up, waving her hand to get rid of the smoke. "Ick, I hate that smell."

Skip pushed a pile of her dirty clothes off the chair on to the floor and sat. "You know," he said, shaking his head, "you're really a piece of work. Here I've been feeling sorry for you because you went psycho again and locked yourself in your room. I was trying to think of a way to get you to come out this morning when I noticed the garden. You've been out there working in it, haven't you?"

Chloe squinted at him. "What?"

"You wait till I leave the house, then you sneak out there with your little rake and hoe, and start planting your stupid flowers."

"You're not making any sense at all," Chloe insisted. "I haven't been out of the house all week."

"Yeah? Well, explain the garden."

This is probably some kind of mean Skip-trick. Chloe walked over to the window. *He's going to laugh when I see how terrible it looks.*

But when she looked out in the back yard, she was dumbfounded by what she saw. Someone *had* been working in the garden. The soil was tilled. Everywhere she looked, little plant shoots were stretching out of their beds in an effort to touch the sky.

It's so green! And so beautiful! Her heart thudded happily. She wiped at the dust covering the window.

"You did this?" she asked Skip.

"No way," Skip said, taking a drag from his cigarette. Then he cocked his head. "What are you saying – that you didn't do this?"

Chloe ran both hands through her hair. "Skip, I swear I haven't been out of this room all week."

He stared at her, exhaling slowly. "You're serious?"

"Completely."

Looking uncertain, he stood up and peered

out the window at the garden. "Maybe you just don't remember it. Maybe you've been sleep-walking."

"Right. Sleepwalking." Chloe pulled on her sneakers and her sunhat and headed for the stairs.

"I ought to call your shrink," Skip shouted, trailing after her. "One second you're lying in here like an invalid, the next you're Mr Greenjeans, farming the land."

"Go ahead and call her," Chloe called over her shoulder.

"She knows you've skipped two sessions. I told her you were sick. Sick is right," Skip said, following her through the kitchen. "In the head. Can't even remember pulling weeds."

Chloe ignored him. The garden's transformation was amazing. *Everything smells so good!* Of course, after being cooped up in that room, almost anything would.

Chloe checked her fingernails. *If I'd been working in the garden, wouldn't there be dirt under my nails? Or did I put on gloves? If I was asleep, would I have thought of that?*

Suddenly, she felt magically alive. *Maybe I have some kind of – secret gardener! Like a fairy godmother, who's come to answer my prayers.*

"Are you listening to me?" Skip demanded.

"Not really," Chloe answered honestly.

"Fine. I've got an interview I have to get to." Skip dropped his cigarette butt on the ground and left in a huff.

Without thinking Chloe knelt and picked up the litter. Besides the wonderful growth of new plants, she noticed that the dogwood had been pruned and the forsythia bushes trimmed. Even the broken sides of the gazebo had been repaired.

A horrifying thought ran through her head. *Could those demons of Mrs Clarkson have worked on this garden? Maybe that's what happened to her. They took over her garden and drove her mad.*

"I've never seen plants like those," a gruff voice broke into her reverie.

Chloe spun and saw Colonel Marquette peering over the fence. She didn't know how to respond. The colonel hadn't been neighbourly the last time she'd talked with him. Far from it.

"Just exactly what are you two growing back there?" he demanded, in a voice that dripped suspicion.

Chloe chose to ignore the colonel. Nothing was going to spoil her new happiness. With a toss of her head, she deliberately turned her back on him and strolled back into her house.

Skip had already gone. Chloe checked the kitchen and living room, appalled by how filthy it had become. Deciding to deal with it later, she went upstairs to her room to get the money she'd kept hidden in her jewellery box. There were a few things she wanted to buy at the garden store.

"Your garden's really starting to look fantastic," Robbie mumbled as he rang up Chloe's new purchases.

"You've seen it?" Chloe asked.

He nodded. "Sometimes I help one of my friends with his newspaper round over there. I saw it this morning." Robbie pointed to the flowering plants in the cardboard box. "These balsams will look really good with what's been started."

"I guess you know what's out there since you sold me the plants."

Robbie shrugged and looked embarrassed. "I recognized most of the flowers, but there are some plants I'm not certain about." Chloe's eyes widened. Maybe Robbie is the secret gardener! *Of course!* Skip had said Robbie liked her. And Robbie admitted he'd been in her garden. *There aren't any demons out there. Just a very shy boy.*

"Robbie, here's a list of items to round up for a phone order," Mrs Helmsley said, coming in from the greenhouse. "You can deliver them this afternoon." Then she noticed Chloe. "Oh. It's you. I didn't see you." Mrs Helmsley raised her chin haughtily and drawled, "I believe I spoke to your neighbour the other day."

"I believe you did," Chloe said, forcing herself to look the woman in the eye. "The colonel told me that you two had talked. He also told me he didn't like living next to a crazy person."

Mrs Helmsley put one hand to her cheek in dismay. "Well, I never intended—"

"You've got the wrong idea about the centre," Chloe interrupted. "No one out there is crazy. Or dangerous."

Mrs Helmsley stared at the keys on her cash register. "That's not what I've heard."

Chloe narrowed her eyes. *Could Mrs Helmsley have been the one who threw the rock through the window?* "The kids just need some guidance and care that they can't get anywhere else," Chloe said. "A few months ago, my mother died and I had nowhere else to go. I was too upset to cope. The centre really helped me."

"I'm sorry about your mother," Mrs Helmsley said, stepping back behind the counter. "But some of those kids on the Monticello tour looked severely disturbed."

"Who looked disturbed?" Chloe asked.

"The boy with the grotesque face, for one," the woman said with a shudder. "Can you imagine him living here – in our neighbourhood?"

Chloe clenched her hands into fists in an effort to maintain control. "Eric is not disturbed. He's just badly disfigured."

"She's right, you know," Robbie declared, boldly. "Some people confuse the two and they really shouldn't."

Mrs Helmsley was floored by Robbie's outburst. "Well, aren't we talkative," she said, arching an eyebrow in his direction.

"Judging Eric by his appearance is as big a mistake as judging you by your accent, Mrs Helmsley," Chloe continued.

"What do you mean by that?" Mrs Helmsley demanded.

"Well, in some parts of the country, people think a Southern drawl is the mark of an ignorant hick. You wouldn't want someone to think that about you now, would you, Mrs Helmsley."

Mrs Helmsley didn't reply. She punched one of the buttons on the cash register with such force that the cash drawer slammed open, hitting her in the stomach.

Robbie gave Chloe a timid thumbs-up behind

Mrs Helmsley's back.

Chloe flushed, imagining Robbie working happily away in her garden.

When she left the nursery, Chloe was so preoccupied with Robbie and the likelihood of him being her secret gardener that she never saw the gang of boys until she was in the middle of them.

They were the same five boys she'd seen at the comic-book shop on her first day in Hamilton. And it was apparent they'd been waiting for her.

She tried to go round, but one of them stepped in front of her. "What's in the bag, loony?"

"Let me go by." Chloe stared at him, trying to ignore the other four circling round her.

One of the boys swatted the bag of supplies out of her arms. She barely managed to hang on to the plants. Several containers of plant food rolled across the sidewalk.

"I'm going to report this to the first policeman I see," Chloe promised.

"Think he'll believe a loony like you?" the boy asked with a nasty grin. "My mom found out about you. There's a lot of us that don't like the idea of living with crazies."

"Hey, Case," one of the others said. "Look at this. Here's a box of bug chow." He made a face.

"Do you think that's what she eats for dinner – worms?"

The boy drew his leg back to kick the rest of her supplies off the sidewalk. Suddenly he was knocked off his feet by someone who bolted into the middle of their circle.

Chloe recognized the stockman's hat at once, but not the sardonic smile that twisted Eric's lips. Fire gleamed in his eyes as he grabbed the boy named Case and flipped him over the boy he'd already thrown to the ground.

Eric set himself in front of Chloe, his hands clenched into fists. One of the boys tried to close in from Eric's blind side, but Eric gave him a backhanded slap that sent him reeling. The impact of flesh on flesh caught everyone's attention.

Case leapt to his feet while another boy helped up the one Eric had slapped. Keeping just out of range, Case waved a forefinger at Eric. "You ugly freak! If you know what's good for you, you won't ever touch me again."

"Do I look like someone who'd know what's good for me?" Eric rasped in a hoarse whisper.

The round-faced manager of the hardware store hurried out, brandishing a broom. "You punks clear out of here before I call the police."

Case and his group withdrew, hurling

invective at Chloe and Eric as they ran.

"You kids OK?" the manager asked.

"Yes, thanks," Chloe nodded.

The manager brought a new paper bag to hold Chloe's plant supplies. In a short time she and Eric had the items rebagged. They stood for a moment in awkward silence.

"Thanks for helping back there," Chloe said. "Those guys are total jerks."

He shrugged and smiled.

Chloe cocked her head. "What are you doing in town, anyway? Was there a group outing?"

Eric shook his head. "I walked to the library."

Chloe blinked in amazement. She'd never known Eric to do that before. The only time he'd ever been to Hamilton was during outings scheduled by Dr Laird.

"I guess I should get home," Chloe said, clutching her bag.

She thought Eric might leave. Instead, he fell in step beside Chloe, keeping the good side of his face towards her.

"What about the group session tomorrow night?" Chloe asked. "Will you be there?"

Eric nodded.

"I heard Doc wants to prepare for the town meeting on Thursday." Chloe sighed. "But I can tell you from personal experience that the chances of a halfway house getting approved by this town are pretty slim. Especially after what's been happening to me."

Eric frowned. "What's happened?"

Chloe quickly told him about the colonel, Mrs Helmsley, and the rock being thrown through their window. She added, "Skip has been absolutely no help in all of this."

Eric nodded sympathetically.

They were standing at a crossing light beside a young mother with three small children. The middle one, who looked about four, was acting like an aeroplane, spinning in circles, not paying any attention to where he was. His mother was trying to get a bottle for the baby in her arms.

Without warning, the little boy stepped off the kerb into the path of an oncoming car. Eric grabbed the boy by the back of his shirt and plucked him from the path of the car with less than a metre to spare.

The boy started crying at once. His mother spun and saw Eric with his hand still gripping the boy's shirt.

"Put my son down!" she screamed. "Don't touch him!" She spun to face the shops. "Help! Someone help me! He's trying to kidnap my son!"

Eric turned the boy loose. The little boy ran to

his mother and wrapped his arms round her legs, nearly causing her to fall.

"Opal!" a black man shouted, running out of the barber's shop behind them. He wore a smock and carried scissors.

Chloe was afraid he was going to attack Eric, so she stepped in front of him.

"Opal, that boy wasn't trying to kidnap Jesse," the barber said. "He just kept him from getting hit by a car. That driver never saw him, and you weren't paying attention. He probably saved Jesse's life."

"Oh." The woman froze. "I'm so sorry. When I saw you – I naturally thought you were trying to hurt my son."

Chloe saw the point of colour burn on Eric's unblemished cheek and got angry. *Now look what you've done.* Eric was just starting to open up but a few careless words had ruined everything.

"Hey Jesse," the oldest boy said, "Two-Face saved you. You know, Two-Face, like in *Batman.* He's the guy with a good face and a bad face."

"Hush William," their mother said. "He can't help the way he looks."

Eric reached up and pulled the brim of his hat lower over his face. Chloe just took his hand and held it. They didn't talk the rest of the way home.

CHAPTER NINE

Chloe let herself into the house and noticed immediately that Skip had been home while she was gone. The usual trail of empty crisp packets and Coke cans were strewn on the floor by the couch.

Evidently Skip had helped himself to the spaghetti left over from weeks before, splattering sauce and parmesan cheese across the kitchen counter, the dining table, and the floors in both rooms. The half-empty sauce container was tipped over in the refrigerator. Thick red sauce had dripped over the two lower racks, then pooled across the glass top of the crisper.

Wonderful. Chloe set her bag of plants on the counter and got a cloth from under the sink. After wetting it, she began to clean the refrigerator.

"So who was that?" Skip asked, appearing suddenly in the doorway. "Your boyfriend?"

Chloe narrowed her eyes at her brother. He must have been watching her from an upstairs window. "That was Eric, if you really want to know. And he's my friend." She shut the refrigerator door and straightened up. "Any more questions?"

"Just one." Skip shook a cigarette out of his pack and put it in his mouth. He continued to stare at her as he fished for his lighter. When he'd finally lit the cigarette, he asked, "What's for dinner."

"I have no idea," Chloe said with a wave of her hand. "I'm not hungry."

Skip took another puff of his cigarette. "Did you eat already?"

"No."

"Then are you sick or something?"

Chloe shook her head and moved out of the kitchen. Skip followed her into the living room. She wrinkled her nose and waved her hand in front of her face. "I'd appreciate it if you wouldn't smoke in here."

"I'll smoke wherever I like," Skip retorted. "I'm paying the bills."

Chloe bit her tongue. *It isn't worth fighting over.*

"So if you're not sick," her brother persisted, pushing a crisp packet aside and flopping on the couch, "what's the problem? Where's dinner?"

"I didn't feel like fixing it."

"Oh, terrific. I'm out all day trying to find a job, and I have to come home and fix my own dinner."

"How did that *big* interview go?" Chloe asked, her voice oozing sarcasm.

"What interview?"

"The one you went on seven hours ago." Chloe folded her arms across her chest. If he wanted to fight, she was ready.

"They already had somebody," Skip said with a shrug.

"Gee, you've been running into that a lot lately," Chloe said, exaggerating her concern.

"What's that supposed to mean?"

She leant towards him. "It means that I don't think you're trying to find a job."

"What would you know about it?" Skip stretched out on the couch and stared at the ceiling. "You've never had to work a day in your life."

"I have to clean up after you constantly," Chloe said, kicking at an old cola bottle on the floor, "and I don't get paid for it."

Skip took a quick drag of his cigarette, exhaling hard. "If it weren't for me, you'd still be in that nuthouse."

"I was happy there," Chloe shouted. "Did that ever occur to you?"

Skip laughed humourlessly. "Who could be happy in a place like that? Talk about Depression City."

"At least everyone there takes responsibility for themselves," Chloe shot back. "Did you even notice the mess you left?"

"I thought the deal was I'd find a job and manage the money," Skip said, ignoring her question, "and you were supposed to take care of the house."

"I don't mind taking care of the house, but cleaning up after you is a waste of time because you never help."

"I don't see you helping bring money into the house."

"If it wasn't for the money Mom left to take care of me," Chloe charged, "you wouldn't have any money."

Skip bolted up and jabbed at the air with his cigarette. "By rights half of that money should have been mine. Instead, it's wasted on those nutcase doctor bills of yours."

"When that money was being spent at the centre," Chloe said, "I was taken care of, I had a nice place to stay, and friends who cared about me. You just want to throw that money away on those jerks you hang out with at the gas station."

"Leon is not a jerk, he's my friend," Skip shot

back.

"If Leon's such a big friend, why doesn't he ever come over to the house."

"Leon really thinks this house is haunted," Skip mumbled. "He believes those stories about Mrs Clarkson and her demons."

Chloe rolled her eyes. "What a total loser."

"*You're* the loser," Skip shouted. "You go and sit with your group of weirdos threes times a week and whine about feeling empty. Man, you don't even know what empty is, until you've been kicked out on the street at age thirteen with no one to go to." His face was purple with anger.

Chloe put her hands on her hips. "What do you mean, kicked out? You went to live with Dad. He didn't want me."

"Dad?" Skip snorted. "Dad took me just to hurt Mom. He got an apartment for him. Said I could sleep on the couch. Which I did, until he threw me out. Said he was tired of me sponging off him."

"Why didn't you just come back to Mom?" Chloe asked, not certain that she could believe his story.

Skip took another drag of his cigarette, and stared at the floor. "He said Mom didn't want me," he said hoarsely. "Told me she begged him to take me off her hands."

Chloe put one hand to her mouth and moaned.

"Oh, Skip, that's just not true. Mom loved you. You don't know how she cried when you left."

Skip slumped against the window frame, looking beaten. His voice was barely a whisper. "I didn't know that until this year."

Chloe suddenly felt chilled. The light had dimmed outside and it was dark inside the house. She took a few steps towards her brother. "But what did you do all those years?"

"Survived." Skip took a final drag of his cigarette and stubbed it out in an old mayonnaise jar lid on the sill. "Sometimes I lived on the street. Sometimes I'd crash at a friend's place. When I worked in Richmond flipping burgers, I actually had my own apartment for a while."

"Then all of those stories about you and Dad doing so many fun things together—"

"Lies." Skip dug in his shirt pocket for another cigarette. "Just to make you feel bad. When I came back home and saw how much you and Mom loved each other, I realized how much I'd missed. I was angry at both of you."

"Did Mom know what had happened to you?"

Skip nodded. "When she got sick, she made an all-out effort to reach Dad. When she got hold of him, he told her he hadn't seen me in years. He did say he heard a rumour I was in Richmond."

"She tried to find you," Chloe said. "That proves how much she loved you."

Skip spun. "Don't you understand? It doesn't matter if she loved me, or not. There was all that time I missed. Time when you were with her, and I was out hustling to just get by." Skip paced the perimeter of the room. "Even after I came back, you wouldn't let me be with her. God, you were always there, ordering me to stop smoking, telling me to get out of her room and let her rest – I barely got to know her. And then she was gone."

Chloe's insides ached as she remembered the day her mother died. Coming home and finding the house empty. "At least you got to say goodbye," she said.

Skip took a deep breath. "Yeah, well, all that's behind us. You can't change the past." He flicked on the living room light.

Chloe blinked at the harshness of the light. Looking across the room, she could see her brother had been crying. Tears streaked his cheeks.

"I don't know about you," he grumbled. "But I'm hungry."

Before Chloe could say another word, he disappeared into the kitchen.

She stood in the living room, feeling a great

sorrow well up inside her. She grieved. For herself. For Skip. She couldn't even imagine how lonely he must have been, spending all those years believing he wasn't wanted.

I should march into that kitchen and tell him I care. Chloe shook her head. *No. I can't. Not yet.*

CHAPTER TEN

The solstice approaches and with it a tantalizing mystery that you're desperate to solve. Something hurts out there and you, Cancer, can heal it. Your keen eye can see into the soul of the situation and smooth over the fragility of another's insecurity.

Chloe sat up.

The old travel clock showed 1.21 a.m. She didn't know what had awakened her.

A cool breeze floated in through the window, dispelling some of the mid-June heat that had baked Hamilton all day. She walked to the window to enjoy the feel of it, then froze when she heard the noise outside.

Heart in her throat, Chloe leaned against the edge of the window and peered out into the garden. At first she couldn't see anything, then a shadow of movement whipping over the wall from the field caught her eye.

I should wake Skip. What if it's a burglar?

But she stayed where she was, hypnotized. As she watched the dark shadow creeping through the garden, Chloe realized the figure was checking the rows of plants. The stalks sticking out of it weren't some eerie appendages at all. The shadow was carrying a rake and a hoe.

Spellbound, Chloe watched as the shadow weeded the rows, taking its time, then began to set out new plants from its pockets. Pruning shears snipped at the trees and bushes, working them into perfection.

Fear mingled with awe thrilled through Chloe as she pulled on her muslin skirt and a T-shirt. She crept downstairs, making as little noise as possible. The story Colonel Marquette had told her about the demons who'd driven Mrs Clarkson crazy filled her head, but she tried to dismiss it.

Whoever's been working in the garden doesn't mean me any harm. If they did, they would have broken into the house. The rationale sounded good as she let herself out of the back door. But on the back step, Chloe paused. *But what if demons are like vampires and can't come into the house unless invited?* She shook her head. *Quit thinking that way.*

Chloe tiptoed as quietly as she could to the edge of the garden, but the shadow heard her. He

– she was sure it was a he – spun round quickly and retreated into the dark shelter of the garden wall. *I wish I'd brought a flashlight.*

He was tall but his shape was blurred by the hooded black cape he wore. His clothing must have been black, too, because nothing caught the weak moonlight streaming through the garden. He kept retreating.

"Don't go," Chloe implored from where she stood. "Please."

The shadow came to a stop about five metres away, partially hidden by the gazebo. "Don't come any closer," a husky male voice whispered.

Chloe strained to hear something recognizable in the phantom's voice, some clue that would identify him. But the breathy whisper obscured it completely.

"Who are you?" Chloe asked, boldly.

"A friend."

"Of me or the garden?"

"At this time of night, where does one begin and the other end?" the shadow asked obliquely.

"Why are you here?"

"You needed help," the shadow said.

"How did you know?"

"I knew."

The voice sounded so eerie, speaking in that

hushed whisper, Chloe took a tiny step forward hoping to get some clue to the phantom's identity. "But why come at night?" she asked.

"So no one would see," the shadow replied. "And because growing things need the moon as much as they need the sun. I tended this garden till the plants found their roots."

"It's beautiful." Chloe took another step.

"Thank you."

Without another word, the shadow withdrew, almost disappearing completely.

"Wait. Don't go."

"Then stay where you are."

"But I just want to know who you are."

"You know who I am. A friend."

"But your name?"

"Ask me no questions and I'll tell you no lies."

"You can't tell me anything more about yourself?"

"No." The phantom paused for a moment, then added, "But I can tell you about these plants." He reached out a hand and touched a plant about twenty-five centimetres high. It had dark green wedge-like leaves and tiny greenish-white flowers. "Do you know what this is?"

Chloe shook her head. "It looks like a weed."

The figured chuckled softly. "That's what

everyone says. But one whiff of this flower's fragrance tells a different tale."

"What's it called?" Chloe asked, fighting the urge to move closer.

"Mignonette."

Chloe tried the word out. "Min-yon-net. It sounds French."

"It is. There is a beautiful story about this rather plain little flower."

With the moon overhead and her mysterious guest whispering dramatically in the shadows, Chloe felt herself being drawn like a magnet into the romance of the moment. "Tell me. Please."

"The story begins – as all good stories do – with the words, 'once upon a time'."

Chloe smiled. Whoever this fellow was, he had a nice sense of humour.

"Once upon a time, there lived a handsome prince in a beautiful castle. This prince would have been lonely were it not for Mignonette—"

"His beautiful princess?" Chloe asked, hopefully.

"I'm afraid not," the stranger replied. "Mignonette was not beautiful. Nor was she a princess. Mignonette was a dwarfish servant girl. She was very sweet and worked very hard to care for the prince, but she was so ugly the prince couldn't bring himself to even look at her.

He would have long conversations with Mignonette but never look her in the face."

"That's sad," Chloe murmured.

"Mignonette didn't mind. The prince was always very kind to her."

Chloe listened intently, loving the sound of the shadow's voice.

"Then one day the prince's castle was attacked by a large band of renegades. The prince, all alone, tried to hold them off. When it looked like defeat was close at hand, the prince stepped into the castle courtyard, ready to die rather than surrender his castle. But the battery of arrows that flew from the ruffians before him did not touch the prince."

"What happened?" Chloe whispered.

"Mignonette, his friend and trusted servant, had thrown herself in front of him. The arrows pierced her poor misshapen body, not his."

"Did she die?" Chloe asked.

"Mignonette died, but the Gods that look down upon us all recognized her true inner beauty. And so there sprouted on the spot where she died a flower as modest in looks as little Mignonette but with a perfume more fragrant than all of the plants in the kingdom."

Chloe closed her eyes and inhaled the fragrance. It smelled intensely sweet, with the faint aroma of raspberries.

"Now, centuries later, this unassuming flower is said to possess magical powers."

"Magic?" Chloe's eyes popped open.

"Those who come under the spell of its perfume are said to have their eyes opened, like the prince's. His were opened too late. Not until the very end did he see the beauty that was inside Mignonette. He mourned her for the rest of his days."

Chloe sighed. "That's a truly sad story."

"It wasn't meant to be."

More than ever Chloe wished she could see who the secret gardener was. But she knew if she tried to move any closer, he would only flee.

"I've got to go," the shadow said finally. "And you need to get some more sleep." He shifted in the darkness.

"Thank you for the story," Chloe said. "And thank you for the garden."

"It was my pleasure," he said.

"This garden saved my life," Chloe confessed. "I was planning to spend the rest of my days locked inside my room."

He chuckled. "You would have found your own reason to come out sooner or later. You're not a quitter, Chloe, no matter how you see yourself. Your friends know." He paused. "I know."

"Will you come back and visit again?"

His silence seemed uncertain.

"Please."

"You have my word." With a soft rustle, he vaulted lithely over the back wall and was gone.

Chloe ran after him, but by the time she pulled herself over the wall the field was empty.

Maybe he is a demon. With all his talk of magical flowers casting spells with their perfume, he could be. Chloe knelt by the mignonette, touching its tiny little flowers and inhaling its rich scent. *Or maybe you're the culprit, little flower. Maybe you've conjured up a mysterious visitor to bring life to my garden – and a garden to my life.*

CHAPTER ELEVEN

The tremolo in operation from Uranus is making you anxious. There seems to be trouble in the air and you don't know why. Old Man Uranus is about to toss a lightning bolt your way – but don't worry, he's only trying to open your eyes to new possibilities. Do be careful crossing streets or crossing paths with ignorant prejudice. You'll prevail if you use a little patience.

"Welcome back, Chloe," Dr Laird called, waving as Chloe got out of the old Toyota. "We've missed you."

The doctor had just parked her car and was standing on the concrete pavement in front of the centre.

Chloe returned the wave, then leant down to talk to Skip, who was behind the wheel. "I'll give you a call when it's time to come and get me," she said. "If that's OK."

"Sure." Skip drummed his thumbs on the

steering wheel. "Uh, Chloe, thanks for dinner tonight. It's the best I've had in over a week."

Chloe smiled, feeling warm inside. "I'm glad. Just save me some of those cookies."

"Now *that* I can't promise." Skip grinned impishly and pulled away.

Chloe walked towards the doctor, feeling better than she had in weeks. She and Skip still hadn't resolved everything, but at least they were talking.

"You two seem to be getting along," the doctor observed as they headed for the front door.

"It's been hard," Chloe admitted, "but I'm starting to see Skip in a different way. I always saw this tough guy, hard as nails, who didn't care about anyone but himself. Now I've discovered—"

"—he's dealing with some of the same abandonment issues you are," Dr Laird said.

Chloe blinked in surprise. "You already knew that."

"That's what the diploma's for," she replied with a smile. "Come on, let's go inside. The meeting is about to start."

A scream ripped across the centre's yard. Chloe turned in time to see a ball of fire flash low across the open space between the brush and the side of the building.

It lit up a man-sized figure hanging from a tree. The scream came again.

"That's Sara," Dr Laird said, breaking into a sprint.

My god, someone's been set on fire! Chloe ran after the doctor, keeping up through sheer adrenaline. At the side of the building, she saw the figure was hanging from a nearby tree, a rope round its neck.

The crawling flames lit up the hanging figure's features: the bulging eyes, the demented smile, the snaggly teeth. All were drawn on the flat surface of the cloth dummy's face. A carving knife, the trademark of dozens of slasher movies, was taped to one of the misshapen hands. The arrow that had set the oil-soaked effigy on fire still quivered in the dummy's chest.

Sara screamed again.

Chloe saw Sara cowering at her open bedroom window, directly across from the tree. Only a few metres away Earl the caretaker stood calmly by, watching.

"Call the fire department!" Chloe screamed.

"Why?" Earl asked with a shrug. "It'll just burn itself out. Ain't nothing to worry about."

Dr Laird ignored the fire and hurried in the side door to help Sara.

"If you won't get the hose, Earl, I will." Chloe dashed for the water hose hanging from the tap near the potting shed. Turning on the tap, she dragged the hose back to the blazing dummy. She had a hard time working the nozzle, but the spraying water started to sluice away the flames. The heat was intense.

Suddenly Earl ripped the hose from her hands. "Let me have that!" He sprayed the dummy down, working from bottom to top. The flames were extinguished in seconds, leaving a sodden mess behind.

"Chloe! Help!"

She turned and saw Matt and Lea coming out of the side door. Matt was weaving unsteadily in his braces, glowing sparks were reflected in his glasses.

"What's wrong?" Chloe called.

"It's Eric," Lea said, pulling at her bulky sweater.

"Where?" Chloe followed them to the back of the building, where they found Eric sitting at the corner. He had his arms wrapped round his knees while he rocked slowly back and forth, staring sightlessly at the dummy.

Oh god. Eric and fire. There's no telling what kind of memories this has unleashed. Chloe knelt beside him and put her hand on his arm.

"Eric." He didn't answer.

"He was coming to help," Lea said. "Then when he saw the figure all wrapped up in the fire, he sat down and hasn't moved or spoken since."

"Help me get him inside." Chloe pulled Eric's arm across her shoulders and made him stand beside her. He didn't look at her, or even seem to be aware of her presence. He was locked up tight inside the nightmares that were more indelible than the scars he wore on his face. Lea took his other side and together they got him moving.

Dr Laird met them in the hall. While she put him to bed, Chloe, Matt and Lea spoke in hushed tones outside his door.

"That fire must have brought back terrible memories," Lea said.

Matt nodded. "Of his father."

"Why his father?" Chloe asked. "Did his dad get burned in a fire, too?"

Lea and Matt looked at Chloe and then each other.

"She doesn't know," Lea murmured.

"Know what?" Chloe grabbed Lea by the arm and pulled her away from Eric's door. "Tell me."

Matt hobbled to join them as Lea said, "Eric's father set him on fire."

"What?" Chloe gasped. "That's terrible. Why?"

"Custody dispute," Lea explained. "Eric's mom and dad had a really messy divorce and she got custody of Eric. On his dad's first visit, he took Eric to a motel, planning to kill himself and Eric."

Matt shoved his glasses up on his nose. "I think he figured if he couldn't have Eric, then nobody could."

"So he set him on fire?" Chloe had never heard anything so horrifying in her life.

"The man was a sicko," Lea said with a shudder.

"The only good news about the whole event is that his father was killed," Matt said. "And Eric lived."

Chloe wrapped her arms round herself and murmured, "Poor Eric."

Matt hobbled to the window to look out at the charred dummy. "I'd like to find out who did this. They must have known how it would affect us."

"It's the CA," Chloe replied. "The Citizens' Alliance doesn't want the halfway house. This is their oh-so-subtle way of telling us to keep out. They threw a rock through my window a couple of weeks ago."

"But what are we going to do about it?" Lea asked. "We can't just let them win without a fight."

Chloe shrugged. Most of the patients at the centre were on very fragile ground struggling to tame their inner fears. The thought of doing battle against an outside enemy was overwhelming.

The ring of the pay phone at the end of the corridor startled all three of them. They just turned and stared. Finally Chloe ran to answer it on the seventh ring. "Hello?"

"You people better stay outta our town." The voice that spoke was harsh and guttural. "Or next time it'll be a *real* dummy that burns." The connection broke with a sharp click.

By the time Chloe returned to the group waiting outside Eric's door, it had grown larger. Katie and Joey were already there, and Sara was moving towards them from her room down the hall.

"What's going on?" Dr Laird asked, as she emerged from inside Eric's room.

In a shaky voice, Chloe related the phone call.

"The town meeting over the halfway house is on Thursday," Dr Laird said. "Evidently someone wants us to just give up without putting the issue to a vote."

"They're not going to scare me away," Matt promised, thrusting his jaw out.

"Personally," Sara said, leaning against the

wall, "I think we'd all be a lot safer if we just stayed here."

The group instantly split into opposing camps. The dissension quickly turned into outright arguments. Despite the doctor's attempts to calm things, the argument only stopped when Earl arrived with the announcement that the police were waiting outside.

"They got some TV cameras out there, too," Earl added. "Hey, you think we'll make the eleven o'clock news?"

"Everyone stay in here," Dr Laird ordered. "We've still got a few days to decide what we're going to do about the halfway house." She started for the door.

"What about Eric?" Chloe asked.

"I gave him something to help him sleep," the doctor said. "He's going to be OK."

"This time," Katie murmured, darkly. "But what happens the next time? And the next? Eric will be a basket case, and who knows what will happen to the rest of us."

Katie dropped into a chair in the front lobby.

"Look, Katie, we won't let that happen," Chloe declared, sitting beside her. "We'll take care of each other. We'll pull together and be strong."

Katie's lips curled into a small smile. "Chloe,

you're a true Cancer. The real care-taker. A loyal friend. Wanting to help everyone. But just remember what happens when the world turns on you – you get your feelings hurt and pull into your shell."

Chloe winced as Katie's words shot through her like the flaming arrow she'd seen outside. That's right, she did run and hide. But not any more. Maybe this time she would stand and fight. She tried to gather her courage, but the flashing red lights whirling across the blinds at the end of the corridor served as a grim warning of what lay ahead.

CHAPTER TWELVE

Cycle is high for creativity, and aspects are excellent for public speaking. Recent events have taught you much about yourself and the people in your life. You have a responsible attitude, and your quiet but impassioned demeanor makes others look as flaky as a pie crust. Carpe diem, *Cancer! You can make a difference.*

"OK, ladies and gentlemen, let's settle down!" The mayor of Hamilton banged his gavel to quiet the voices filling the high school auditorium. He was a beefy, broad-faced man, with grey hair and a handlebar moustache. "Order, please!"

Chloe looked round. The staff and kids from the centre had been seated near the back of the room, a position Chloe felt had been deliberately chosen to intimidate them. The auditorium was crowded with people, and on the other side of the room a few carried placards that proclaimed

NO HALFWAY HOUSES FOR HALFWITS and **KEEP HAMILTON SANE AND SAFE.**

"I guess the battle lines have been drawn clearly enough," Dr Laird whispered angrily from her seat beside Chloe.

Chloe noticed Mrs Helmsley and Colonel Marquette sitting with other members of the Citizens' Alliance group. She was surprised to see Robbie Proctor seated a few rows behind them, but he blushed and waved when she caught his eye. Chloe cocked her head, trying to imagine him in a cape in her moonlit garden. The previous night Chloe had waited at her window until after one o'clock in the morning, hoping to see her phantom again but he hadn't appeared. Of course, it was a little much to expect him to work in her garden every night. After all, he had a day job at Helmsley's nursery.

"Hey," Lea murmured beside her, "isn't that Skip?"

Chloe turned in the direction indicated. Sure enough, Skip was standing at the back of the room, an open can of soda in his hand. He was talking to Leon from the service station.

"Yes, that's him," Chloe said.

"What's he doing here?"

"I don't know. He never said a word about coming." Though they'd been getting along better at home, Chloe hadn't talked to her brother about the town meeting. However, Skip had been at home when Dr Laird arrived in the centre's bus to pick her up.

After the treasurer's report and the minutes from the last meeting were reviewed, the mayor got down to business. He outlined the situation, stating that Barrett Centre was prepared to sue the town for discrimination if it refused to sell them a home. Then he opened the floor for discussion. Colonel Marquette was first to be recognized.

The colonel was resplendent in his military full dress uniform. He took the podium with confidence.

"Makes me want to salute," Matt said behind Chloe.

Not me. Chloe knew the colonel had only worn the uniform to impress the townspeople with what a hard-working patriot he was. But Chloe didn't buy it.

"Halfway houses don't work," Marquette barked into the microphone. "How many times have we seen on the news a story about some mentally deranged kid showing up at a playground or school with a gun, with tragic results? It's bad enough we have to live in fear of them escaping from that centre, but to just let them loose, free to do as they please in our neighbourhoods, is too much."

Heads were nodding in the audience

"We live in dark times," the colonel went on, "where young people are no longer taught the difference between right and wrong. Where sick children murder their own parents in their sleep. Yes, they need our help and compassion. But that doesn't mean we have to be foolhardy and put our community, our own families, at risk. What's going to stop these teenagers from hurting perfect strangers? The only safe place for them is behind the walls of an institution."

Some of the listeners cheered their support of Colonel Marquette.

"And what does this centre and its staff really contribute to our community?" Marquette charged. "Sure, they shop at local stores, and they employ a few local people. But does that meagre amount justify putting our own selves in harm's way? It does not!"

The colonel left the podium to loud applause from about half of the audience. The mayor quickly introduced Dr Laird, calling her Ms Laird and stripping her of her professionalism.

Chloe was proud to see the doctor take it all in her stride. She promptly set the record straight, making sure the secretary got it down that she was *Doctor* Laird. Then she addressed the assembly.

"Is there anyone in this room who's never had a problem they've had trouble coping with?" the doctor challenged.

At first it didn't look like anyone was going to reply. Then Colonel Marquette stood. "I think we've all had our share of problems, ma'am. But we faced them down."

"Alone?" Dr Laird asked.

"Yes, ma'am. I think so."

"Do you, Colonel?" The doctor shifted all of her attention to Marquette. "Have you been in combat?"

Marquette appeared unflinching. "Several times."

"Were you prepared for that experience?"

"Yes, ma'am."

"And who prepared you?"

"I prepared myself. When the day came, I was one of the first soldiers off the boat."

"Very commendable, Colonel." Dr Laird moved out from behind the podium. *She doesn't want anyone to get the idea that she's hiding.* "But didn't you have instructors in boot camp."

"Yes, ma'am," Marquette answered proudly, his chest puffing visibly. "The meanest drill sergeants in the Corps."

"Would you say they helped you develop your inner strengths, and find the discipline to master your weaknesses?" the doctor asked.

"Yes, ma'am."

"Then I wouldn't call them drill sergeants," Dr Laird said smoothly. "I'd call them counsellors." Marquette started to say something, but she cut him off, turning her attention deliberately to another section of the audience. "Thank you, Colonel. You may sit down."

Surprisingly, the colonel did, though stiffly.

"You see, life is a lot like war," Dr Laird continued. "You've got to plan and struggle and retrench every day to survive. Some of us try to fight it without the proper information. Intelligence, as it's called in the military. And some of us try to fight it without the proper tools." She gazed round the auditorium.

No one said anything, though the people carrying the signs shifted nervously.

"So, to use the Colonel's way of thinking, I guess you could think of me as the Barrett Centre's drill sergeant. I train my people to take responsibility for themselves in the battle of life. I inform them and equip them. And I can guarantee you that I don't allow any loose cannons on my ship. I also don't let my squad out of boot camp until they're ready. But now I've got several who *are* ready to strike out on their own, to join the other citizens of Hamilton as productive, responsible members of the community. Now that we have the funding, we shouldn't be kept waiting."

Chloe and several kids from the group applauded. She saw many heads in the audience nodding in approval.

"As the mayor mentioned earlier, the centre has a lawyer already on retainer who's ready to fight for us. I'm sure *60 Minutes* or some other programme wouldn't mind taking a ringside seat at our court battle, if it comes to that."

A wave of rumbling swept through the audience.

"Are you threatening us?" Mrs Helmsley demanded.

Dr Laird shook her head. "I'm simply stating what will happen should this go to court. The staff at Barrett Centre are not going to back down on this issue. I want there to be no confusion about that."

The grumbling grew louder, and Dr Laird held up her hands. "But it doesn't have to be that way. I believe in these kids, and they believe in me. They don't frighten me because I know them intimately. To you they're strangers, and it's a sad fact of human nature that we are usually suspicious and afraid of what we don't know. So why don't we get better acquainted with one other?" She looked at Chloe and the others. "Would you kids please come up here for just a moment, and introduce yourselves?"

Chloe got up, her hands shaking slightly. Though some of the kids had agreed to speak, it was certainly more scary walking up to do it than talking about it.

When they reached the platform, Lea spoke first. "My name is Lea. I'm anorexic. For those of you who don't know what that means, anorexia is an eating disorder. I think I'm too fat, so I don't eat." Her lip trembled as she said, "A year ago, I was near death. Dr Laird helped bring me back to life. Doc and the kids at the centre are helping me learn to like myself. I have good and bad days." She looked round the room. "Probably like all of you. I know I'm not perfect and I'm learning to live with that, but I think I'm ready to be a productive member of this community." She paused. "I'd really appreciate it if you'd give me that chance. I'm not a bad person. Honest."

Chloe had tears in her eyes as Lea stepped back and joined the others. Judging from the people she could see, Lea's words had had a sobering effect on the audience.

Matt spoke next. "My name is Matt," he said, gripping the sides of the podium as little beads of sweat broke out on his brow. "I'm twelve years old and I'm not a murderer. I don't think I've ever even met a murderer. My big problem is my legs – I have trouble walking, and I have to wear these braces." He slapped the braces on his legs. "The doctors tell me I will probably be in a wheelchair in another couple of years. I hope not. But they've always been right before..." Matt stopped and looked down at the podium. He bit his lip hard, then faced the audience once more. "Doc is helping me adjust to that possibility, but it's hard. At Barrett Centre, we can't have any animals. I was told we could at the halfway house. I'd really like to have a puppy to play with, and chase, and take for long walks, while I can still move my legs. Thank you."

Matt's innocent eyes seemed larger than ever, blinking solemnly from behind his magnifying lenses. The auditorium had grown very quiet. Chloe noticed several women dab their eyes. A few men cleared their throats.

Then it was Chloe's turn to speak. She threw her shoulders back and tried to look confident. *Please don't let my voice crack, or do anything to make them think I'm a crazy person.* "My name is Chloe Summerlin. I'm currently living in a house on Delaney Street with my brother, Skip. I was at the centre because I lost my mother in the spring after a long illness. She was everything to me, and when she died, I - I had trouble coping with the loss. I sort of folded up and went away inside myself for a long time.

At the time of Mom's death, I had no family to live with so I was sent to the centre. I am very grateful that I was placed in such a loving, nurturing environment. Every day is a struggle because I miss my mother terribly. But my brother, Skip, has come back home, and we're going to try to help each other get through this together."

Some of the signs on the Citizens' Alliance side were coming down.

"Colonel Marquette is my neighbour," Chloe continued. "When I first moved in, he seemed interested in getting to know me. During the times I talked with him, I found out he was a retired military man, that his wife Eunice has asthma and donates time to the Red Cross and other charities in Hamilton. I know they have three children who are successful and have made them grandparents five times over."

"If I know the colonel," someone commented

loudly, "she's had to suffer through looking at those grandkids more than once." Laughter rippled through the audience. Even Colonel Marquette cracked a smile.

Chloe focused her eyes on the colonel. "I picked up supplies from the garden shop for you and even lent you a stamp when you needed to mail a letter. I think you really enjoyed our conversations, Colonel. Why, you even told me you thought I was a very nice young person. One you'd like your grandson to meet."

The colonel stared back at Chloe impassively.

"But the second you found out I was an outpatient at the centre, you threatened to have me and my brother kicked out of our house. You didn't bother to find out what had happened to me, or why I needed the centre – you just wanted me thrown out on the street." Chloe turned back to the rest of the audience. "So I ask you, if you could live next to me or Colonel Marquette – who would you choose?"

Scattered applause followed Chloe off the stage. Robbie gave her a thumbs up. She even saw Eric nodding in approval from his seat in the very back row. The colonel looked furious but sat stiffly in his seat, arms crossed, his face as hard as stone.

Skip was in the kitchen when Chloe got home. Doc had taken everyone for pizza after the meeting. Instead of the usual soft drink, he was holding a beer. Half a dozen empties and an over-flowing ashtray sat on the counter.

"Big night?" Chloe asked, pouring herself a glass of iced tea. She glanced out in the garden but there were no shadows stirring in the darkness.

"Celebrating," Skip said. "You did good up there, sis. You really nuked the colonel. Even Leon thought so."

"Did Leon come over here afterwards?" Chloe got a plastic garbage bag from beneath the sink and started clearing the counter.

"Only for a minute. He says this place gives him the creeps. But we were both celebrating." He glanced at her. "Lighten up. It's just a couple of beers."

"Drinking makes me nervous."

"Then leave it to me."

Chloe didn't smile.

"Joke," Skip told her. He finished his beer and tossed the bottle in the trash. "It's only beer. I can handle it, and I'm not going to be driving tonight anyway."

"Would you like something to eat?"

"No. We stopped for a burger on the way home."

That's what I saw in the living room. Then Chloe noticed her photo albums spread across the dining table. "Skip, those are my albums."

"I know." Skip walked over to the table. "I hope you don't mind me getting them out, but I just wanted to look." He flipped through the pages. "There are a whole lot of people in here I haven't seen in years."

Chloe looked at the page he was staring at. "You know them?" She'd studied those pictures for months, but they were mysteries her mother had never unravelled.

"Sure. These are Dad's relatives." Skip nodded. "I guess you don't remember seeing them, do you?"

"No."

"You were pretty little." Skip turned the page. "Don't worry. You didn't miss much. Every one of them is just like Dad – self-centred and pig-headed." He tapped one of the photos thoughtfully. "You know, I figured I was bucking the odds when I came back here to see you. You don't have any idea how much I've wanted a family. You and Mom were the only two people I ever felt even sort of close to. But I knew you didn't like me much."

Chloe started to object.

Skip shook his head. "I don't blame you. I can

kind of wear on the nerves. When you hid out in your room last week, I thought it was over. Poof! No more family. I figured we were just carrying on some kind of family curse." He looked at her. "But you're pulling yourself together, sis. And now, I am too. Because tonight, I landed a job."

Chloe's face brightened. "Really?"

"Really." Skip crossed his heart and held up his right hand. "You're looking at the new night watchman for Quality Appliances. I start tomorrow night."

"That's great!" Before she knew it, Chloe had crossed the distance between them and hugged Skip.

He seemed awkward about the sudden show of emotion, and hugged her gently in return. "Leon at the service station recommended me for the job. See? He's not so bad after all."

Chloe reached into one of the cabinets and pulled out a cannister. "We have something else to be happy about," she said, wiggling her eyebrows. "I hid the last batch of m&m cookies. There's at least six for you and six for me."

"All right!" Skip hooted with laughter, giving her a high-five. "Let the celebration begin."

CHAPTER THIRTEEN

You've had a secret fear of not having money. Something in your past was taken away from you, and now you're afraid someone is out to grab whatever you've got left. And Cancer will hold on with those claws! But lighten up – there isn't a thief in the whole solar system.

"You're smiling. You must be happy."

Chloe looked up at Robbie Proctor as he walked behind the counter at Helmsley's to ring up her purchases.

"I am," she said, feeling her cheeks flush pink. With Skip's new job now five days old, they weren't quite as worried about money as they had been. The garden was doing so well that she couldn't resist adding a few more plants.

"My counsellor, Dr Laird, called me this afternoon and told me the halfway house has been approved. We're just waiting for a site."

"Sounds great," Robbie said, boxing her plants. "I'm happy for you guys. My mom was out at the centre once, and she talked about your group for days. She's always telling people they don't realize how easy they've had it. She's fully supportive of the halfway house."

"If she's a real estate agent," Chloe said with a smile, "then we're in business."

Robbie shook his head. "Sorry. She's an accountant and works for the state." He passed Chloe her plants, then looked at something behind Chloe. "Hey, you don't have any of this in your garden." He walked round the counter and picked up a plant with thick white flowers.

"It's pretty," Chloe conceded, running her fingers through the leaves. "But I've forgotten the name. What's it called?"

"Sweet alyssum," Robbie said. "Many formal gardens use them as borders. It's still early enough to plant some and you'll have have blooms until the first few frosts."

"I don't have any more money to spend."

Robbie shrugged. "Then let it be my gift to you. I've always been partial to alyssum in a garden, and I like the name." He chuckled and added, "When I first started working here, I read the tag wrong and called it, 'sweet asylum'. Which is exactly what a well-kept garden feels like to me."

Sweet asylum? Chloe cocked her head and

looked at Robbie once again, picturing him in a cape. He was tall enough to be her secret gardener, and he certainly liked gardening. *You're also shy enough not to want to be known.*

Outside, Chloe walked towards home. A horn honked twice and she looked over at the service station. Skip was there in the Toyota, talking to Leon. He was on his way to his job at Quality Appliances and Electronics. He waved and she waved back, feeling warm and fuzzy.

It's been a long time since you've felt this happy. Now, if her secret gardener showed up later, it would be a perfect night. For the past four nights he hadn't appeared. Chloe had set her alarm and waited for a couple of hours each night. Each time she'd gone back to bed disappointed.

She glanced at the stars peeking out of the darkening sky overhead. He'd be there eventually, she was certain. After all, he told her he would return. She was surprised at how much she wanted to speak to him again.

"Chloe."

Startled, she almost jumped out of her skin. It was well after one o'clock in the morning. She must have dozed off, waiting in the garden.

When she turned, she saw the shadow near the gazebo.

"I was beginning to think you weren't coming back," she scolded gently. "It's been almost a week."

"But it's been a busy week," the caped figure whispered.

Chloe tried to make out more details about him, but the black cape softened and distorted all the lines. His face was masked by the hood. "What have you been doing?"

"Sleeping, mostly. These late nights have taken their toll." He laughed softly.

"Would you like something to eat or drink?"

"No. Thank you." He took a few paces round the garden, but remained careful to keep a distance from her. "The garden looks good. You've been working hard."

"It's taking much less work. I'm just maintaining it."

The shadow crouched near the sweet alyssum she'd put in only a few hours ago by flashlight. The flowers looked stark white in the full moon. "Sweet alyssum."

"It can look like sweet asylum if you read the tag wrong," Chloe hinted.

He didn't take the bait. "Yes. I guess it does."

The silence lingered between them for a

moment. "Tell me who you are," Chloe begged.

"I can't."

"I'm dying to know."

He straightened and, though she couldn't see his eyes, she could feel them on her. "Maybe I should stop coming."

"No!" she said quickly. "Why won't you tell me who you are? I feel I know you so well already. But I want to know everything about you."

"This is the best I can offer," he said. "For now."

"Will you visit again?"

"I don't know. Things are – difficult. I hadn't planned on you finding me here. And I really didn't think I'd be returning to speak to you. I should have stayed away." He paused. "But I couldn't. I'm weaker than I thought. Or maybe the darkness is making me more bold than I have any right to be."

"Don't be afraid of me," Chloe said softly.

"I'm not."

She took a step closer, waiting to see if he would move. He didn't. She took another step. He still didn't.

"I'm afraid of me," he whispered hoarsely.

"Don't be." Chloe's voice grew hushed as she continued to move slowly forward.

The distance between them diminished to several metres, then to only one. He looked solid and powerful standing before her. The night chill caught his breath in soft puffs of mist that the breeze pulled away. She raised her hand. In a heartbeat she'd be able to touch his face beneath the hood.

"No!"

His voice was choked with pain. In a whirl of blackness, he spun and ran for the back wall.

"Don't!" Chloe begged, running after him. "Please don't leave me!"

Why couldn't you have just left things alone? You should have gone slower. You knew he was afraid. You knew it.

When she reached the stone wall, he had already vanished.

She didn't know how long she stood at the wall, hoping he would come back. *What if he doesn't? What if he never comes back?*

The possibility made her ache inside.

Across town, Chloe heard the plaintive wail of sirens. Defeated, she let go of the wall and walked back to the house. She'd have to wait and see. There was nothing more she could do.

CHAPTER FOURTEEN

You can't quite figure out the purpose of this phase in your life. Remember, a minor setback is only that. Tonight Uranus sticks out his tongue at Neptune and thumbs his nose at the Moon. You must have the confidence to go ahead with your plans, even though others seem bent on discouraging you.

The next morning, the harsh ringing of the telephone cut through Chloe's sleep. She found the phone with a flailing hand, then brought it to her ear. "Hello."

"It's Lea. Chloe, you'd better come to the centre."

"What?" Chloe blinked her gritty eyes and tried to wake up. The travel alarm told her it was almost nine.

"The police are here. There was a robbery in town last night. They got an anonymous tip and found some of the stolen goods stashed at the centre."

"You're kidding." Chloe got out of bed and started dragging clothing out of her closet.

"So now they think one of the patients at the centre committed the robbery. Doc is talking to the police, but it doesn't look good."

"I'm on my way."

Chloe said goodbye and hung up. As soon as she was dressed she went to Skip's room to ask him for a ride. But he wasn't there. He wasn't downstairs, either, and the car wasn't in the driveway. Usually he was home no later than seven-thirty. She called the taxi service, then raided the cookie jar for their emergency money.

On the way through town Chloe asked the cabbie to stop at Helmsley's garden stores. She wanted to talk to Robbie, to see if he might have seen Skip that morning or knew anything about the robbery. She also wanted to know if he looked as if he hadn't had any sleep last night. She felt certain that he was her secret gardener. *Maybe if I tell him I know, he'll admit it.*

But the girl behind the counter told Chloe that Robbie wasn't coming in today.

Chloe wanted to ask more questions, but Mrs Helmsley appeared from the back and the tension between them was too much to bear. Instead, Chloe said thanks and went back out to the waiting taxi.

Police cars were blocking the circular drive at the centre, so Chloe got the taxi to drop her in the parking lot. She raced across the drive and into the building.

"Some of these kids have got no business having out-patient privileges," Earl the caretaker was saying to the two uniformed cops in the entranceway. "If it was up to me, I'd never let any of them out. Look what happens. Believe me, I could tell you stories about this place."

Lea met Chloe by the reception desk and led her back into the dormitory area, away from Earl. "This place is a zoo," Lea whispered. "Sara's barricaded herself in her room and is refusing to talk to anyone, in spite of the fact that the police aren't interested in her at all. Matt's creeping through the halls playing detective, certain he's going to catch the people responsible."

"What about Katie? How's she doing?"

"She's in an up period," Lea said. "She's running round like a giddy lunatic, thoroughly enjoying the intrigue. None of them truly understands that this is serious. I mean, the police found CD players and microwaves – big ticket items."

Chloe nodded. "Well, it does seem like some

kind of practical joke. I mean, none of us would ever steal anything." She paused and leant closer. "With the exception of Kelly Raiford."

"But Kelly's just a dime store variety kleptomaniac," Lea said. "Things she could slip in her pocket. Not like the stuff they found."

"Where's Doc?" Chloe asked, peering into the television room.

"Still talking to the cops." Lea led Chloe into her bedroom and closed the door.

"They really think someone here was responsible for the robbery?" Chloe asked, sitting on her old bed across from Lea's.

"Oh yeah." Lea nodded vigorously. "If they can't prove we were all in it together, they're going to settle for just hanging one of us."

I really hope she's exaggerating. But Chloe knew that the crisis was real. She could see the chances of getting their halfway house rapidly diminishing.

A knock sounded on the door. "I know you're in there, Chloe. Isn't this exciting?"

Lea rolled her eyes at Chloe. "Come on in, Katie."

Katie opened the door a crack and stuck her head inside. "Robberies, police, an unknown suspect – Matt and I are working together. We're going to crack this case."

"These people aren't playing round," Chloe reminded Katie. "One of us will be arrested if we're not careful."

Katie dropped her perky façade for just a moment. "I'm well aware of that, Chloe. And being a Cancer, you should understand that we all have to work on this in our own way. Use your imagination, Chloe. We're counting on you to help us."

With those strange words of wisdom, Katie shut the door.

Lea stared hard at Chloe. "Katie's right. We all need to use our imaginations. We're smart. We can figure this out."

Chloe nodded. "Let's start at the beginning. You said the stolen goods they found here were big. Like what?"

"Electronics stuff, mostly." Lea waved her hand absently. "Computer equipment. Printers. Fax machines. A couple of cellular phones. Some radar detectors. A microwave oven."

Someone knocked on the door. Lea opened it to find the doctor standing there.

"Nancy told me you were here," Dr Laird said to Chloe.

"I called her," Lea admitted.

"It's OK," the doctor said, patting Lea on the shoulder. She turned to Chloe. "You've been told what's going on?"

"Yes," Chloe said. "But it's ridiculous. That stuff they found? How could anyone living here hope to use any of it? No one has a computer or a car or a phone."

"It seems clear to me that someone planted that evidence to discredit the centre," the doctor replied. "But the police are being pressured to do something quickly. The word leaked out about the stolen merchandise being found here and some people in town are demanding action."

Chloe wrinkled her nose. "The Citizens' Alliance."

Dr Laird sighed wearily. "Exactly."

"What are we going to do?" Lea asked.

"Let the police do their job," Dr Laird replied, "and try to keep this incident from hurting us. Chloe, I have a favour to ask. You and Eric seem to be getting along. He's spoken to you more than anyone else here."

Chloe shrugged. "He probably talks most to Matt."

Dr Laird nodded. "Yes, but you're the adult he trusts." She paused. "Eric is in his room. The police want to talk to him, but he's being uncooperative. He won't even respond to me. When I heard you were here, I thought maybe you wouldn't mind giving it a try."

"Why do the police want to talk to him?" Lea asked.

The doctor's face drew tight. "Someone told the police they saw Eric in town last night at the time the robbery occurred. I'm afraid they intend to arrest him."

"They can't do that! Eric's no thief!" Chloe cried.

"Then please, try to help."

A tense Chloe followed Dr Laird down the hallway to Eric's room.

He lay in a foetal position on his bed, staring fixedly at a point on the wall. He seemed oblivious to everything round him. Doc left Chloe in the room.

"Eric," Chloe said, "can we talk?"

He ignored her. With his unblemished cheek towards her, Eric looked young and vulnerable.

"I know you didn't have anything to do with that robbery last night," Chloe said. "Everyone here at the centre knows that. All you have to do is tell the police you were here."

He remained silent, not looking at her.

"Eric, it seems to me we have two choices. We can let the world walk over us, which seems like the easiest choice – at first. Or we can just say no, I'm not going to be treated that way. A few weeks ago, I was about to opt for choice one, when a special friend helped me see that wasn't a good idea."

Eric stared at the wall and muttered, "You had a choice. People look at my face and make the choice for me."

"Eric, please..."

The sound of her voice made him pull himself into a tighter ball. Only too well, Chloe knew he had shut her, and everything else, out of his world.

Chloe left the room and pulled the door closed behind her. "He won't talk to me either," she whispered to Dr Laird.

Both of them turned to watch a burly police officer approach from down the corridor. "This where the Irons kid is?"

"Yes," the Dr said.

"I'm going to have to talk to him. Your caretaker just confirmed that Eric was AWOL last night."

Dr Laird's eyes widened. "You're sure?"

"Yep." The sergeant nodded. "We're going to move quickly on this because the stuff we found here was just a fraction of what was stolen. If we can't track it soon, very little of it will ever get returned to Quality Appliances."

"Quality Appliances?" Chloe echoed, suddenly feeling afraid.

"Right. They were hit last night at about one-thirty."

"But my broth—" Chloe suddenly clapped a hand over her mouth. She didn't want to drag Skip into this unless she had to. *But if he was the night watchman – where was he when the robbery occurred?*

"We need to find out who this Eric kid was working with before they get the stolen property out of state," the sergeant explained to the doctor. "We suspect a gang working across state lines, possibly with an Atlanta or DC connection. But that kid has to tell us what he knows – and quick."

Chloe excused herself and went to find a phone. Eric was facing possible arrest and her brother was missing. *I hope nothing has happened to Skip!*

CHAPTER FIFTEEN

Chloe's mind whirled during the taxi ride home. Although the police hadn't formally arrested Eric, they'd left a man at the centre on guard outside his door. Dr Laird was not happy, but there was nothing she could do about it.

And although Chloe had called home several times and let the phone ring as many as thirty times, Skip had never answered. *What if whoever robbed Quality Appliances took him out somewhere and shot him?*

Chloe could feel the panic rising inside her. It was taking every ounce of her strength to keep a lid on her emotions. She kept reminding herself she needed to think clearly. If she was going to help her friends, and her brother, she couldn't allow herself to be side-tracked by fear.

As the taxi neared her house on Delaney street Chloe spied the beat-up old Toyota parked in the driveway.

"Skip's car!" she cried out in relief. "He's safe!"

She paid the fare and rushed into the house.

Skip was curled up in a blanket on the couch, asleep. He was still fully dressed in his guard uniform. The silver Thermos Chloe had bought him as a gift for getting the job was clutched in one hand.

"Skip." Chloe shook him hard. "Skip, wake up!"

He groaned and looked up at her blearily. "Hey, take it easy. I'm sleeping." He wiped at his red-rimmed eyes. "Leave me alone."

"Skip!" Chloe shouted. "Wake up this instant!"

Startled, Skip pulled himself to a sitting position. "What? What? Why are you shouting?"

Chloe was starting to get a little angry. She folded her arms across her chest. "I thought you were dead!"

Skip put his head in his hands. "Don't talk so loud. I've got a headache that would bring King Kong to his knees."

Chloe wouldn't let up. "What's the matter with you? Have you been drinking?"

Skip continued to hold his head. "Of course not. But it sure feels like it." He pressed the base of skull gently. "Whoa. It's just throbbing, right here. I need a cup of coffee."

He fumbled for the Thermos that had fallen on its side on the couch. "I'm in luck. It's practically full."

Chloe watched as he poured some into the plastic top that doubled as a cup. His hands were shaking. "When did you get home?"

Using both hands to hold the cup steady, Skip brought it to his lips. "I guess I got home at the usual time."

"You don't remember?" Chloe narrowed her eyes, suspiciously.

"Not really, no," he muttered, taking a deep sip.

"Skip, listen to me." Chloe spoke slowly and clearly. "When I left the house this morning after nine, you weren't home. And sometime during the night, Quality Appliances was robbed."

"Quality was robbed?" Skip jerked his head up so hard, the coffee spilled all over the front of him. "Yeow! Geez!" He leapt off the couch. "When?"

"Round one-thirty in the morning," Chloe replied. "So where were you?"

"I was there. I promise." He rubbed his head. "I just don't remember anything."

Terrible seeds of doubt were taking root inside Chloe. *Could Skip have been involved with the robbery?* "Sirens went off, the police were all over the place." She couldn't keep the sarcasm out of her voice. "So why is it the night watchman, whose job is to *prevent* things like this, has no memory of a full-blown robbery?"

Skip looked at her blankly. "I don't know, Chloe. Now that I think about it, I really don't remember a thing about the entire night."

Calm, Chloe, just keep everything calm. "What's the last thing you remember?" she asked.

"Punching the time clock at midnight." He shook his head. "After that, it's all a blur."

"What did you do before you went to work last night?"

Skip shrugged. "Hung out with Leon at the gas station. The usual."

Chloe chewed thoughtfully on her lower lip. "Was anything strange last night? Were you sick before you went in?"

"No. I felt fine." Skip poured himself another cup of coffee from the Thermos. He paused and turned the Thermos in his hand. "That's odd."

"What?"

"Well, I usually burn through this Thermos of coffee in the first hour, but it looks like I never even touched it."

Chloe picked up the Thermos. "That means that something must have happened to you before you could even take a drink."

Skip rolled his head in a circle to get out the kinks in his neck. "I just don't understand this. If the store was robbed, I would have been there. But I don't remember talking to the police."

"And they haven't called or come out here since you got home?"

Skip shook his head. "They may not have known I was even working there. Mr Fedderson, Quality's owner, hired me just before he went out of town and didn't tell anyone because he was concerned about some internal thefts. He thought I might nab someone easier if they didn't know about me. But he's on vacation and not due back in till next week."

Chloe sat on the couch next to Skip. "If the police never spoke to you, then that means you weren't at the warehouse."

"But I was!" Skip protested. "I had to be. I distinctly remember driving over there." He shook his head in frustration. "I just don't remember leaving."

"Maybe you didn't leave there. Maybe someone knocked you out and removed you before the police got there."

"But who?" Skip asked, squinting one eye shut and peering at Chloe.

Chloe's eyes suddenly widened. "Can you

drive?" she asked.

"I think so," Skip nodded. "This coffee seems to have helped. But where are we going?"

Chloe stood up. "To see Leon."

"Leon? Whatever for?"

Chloe was already headed for the door. "He was the last person you spoke to before you blacked out. Do you know where he is right now?"

Skip checked his watch. "He's got the morning shift at the station today. But do we really need to talk to Leon? This is really embarrassing. He's going to think I'm a total loser."

Chloe spun and pointed at her brother. "Look at yourself, Skip. You're barely functioning. If you don't remember last night and don't remember getting home, that makes me think someone must have drugged you. Maybe Leon saw something."

"Oh." Skip fumbled in his pocket for his keys. "OK. Well, let's go then."

Leon wasn't at the station when they arrived a few minutes later. The other attendant told them he was on lunch break. They could find him at the Catawba Café next door. Chloe thanked him for the information and she and Skip walked over to the cafe. Her brother had taken several aspirin but continued to nurse a cup of coffee.

The café was small and homey, made dark by the pulled blinds. Standing in the alcove by the entrance, Chloe peered round the booths for Leon while Skip bought a pack of cigarettes from the vending machine. She recognized Leon's hat first.

"There he is." Chloe reached for Skip, about to pull him along when she noticed who was sitting with Leon.

Grinning and slapping Leon on the back was Earl Levitt, the caretaker from Barrett Centre.

"Don't move," Chloe hissed. She flattened herself against the wall, yanking Skip back with her. "Do you see who Leon's with?"

Skip peeked round the alcove. "Sure. His cousin, Earl." Skip lit a cigarette and fanned away the smoke. "Some nights Earl hangs out with us at the station."

"Let's go." Chloe pushed Skip back towards the door.

"I thought we were going to talk to Leon," he protested.

"I don't think we need to any more," Chloe said. "Now get in the car before they see us."

Skip slid behind the Toyota's steering wheel. "You want to give me a clue as to what's going on here, sis?"

Chloe's mind worked furiously, putting together the pieces of the puzzle. "Leon got you the job at Quality, and Earl works at the centre. Your last stop before going to work last night was Leon's gas station. Were both of them there?"

Skip took a drag of his cigarette, thinking. "Yes."

Chloe stared hard at her brother. "Now think, Skip. Tell me every little thing that happened."

"Well, Leon had asked me to stop by the station before work because he wanted to show me this new sports car he was working on. I drove over and we looked at it."

"Did you eat anything?"

Skip shook his head. "Not from the station. Just a Snickers bar I brought from home."

"How about a Jolt cola? Did you drink one of those?"

"Didn't need to. Leon had just made a fresh pot of coffee. Told me it was high octane – guaranteed to keep my eyelids open for the whole night..." Skip turned to Chloe, his eyes huge. "The coffee."

Chloe nodded, excitedly "OK, we're on a roll. You go to work, and Earl and Leon follow you. The drug Leon put in the coffee is starting to work and you don't even notice them follow you into the building."

"I pass out," Skip said, rubbing the sore spot on the back of his head.

"And Leon and Earl loot the place while you're unconscious. They take you out with them. Then, using Earl's keys, they plant some of the merchandise at the centre. And finally they set off the alarm back at the appliance store." Chloe held out her arms, palms up. "The police get an anonymous tip from Earl, find the goods – and Earl and Leon are in the clear."

Skip frowned. "But why would they do that to me?"

"Because they're scumballs," Chloe said flatly. "They used you."

Skip took another drag of his cigarette. "But what's the point of stashing the goods at the centre?"

Chloe raised one finger. "They didn't put all the goods there. Just enough to pin the crime on the patients. They know how upset the town is about the halfway house. Lots of people here will be eager to believe that some loony broke into Quality Appliances. Then they could say I-told-you-so."

Skip let out a big cloud of smoke. "So the question is – where's the rest of the loot?"

"Do you know where Leon lives?"

"Yeah. But if you're thinking about going over there to check this out, there's no way I'm going to let you do that."

"Skip," she said softly, "you realize that once the police find out about you, they're going to suspect you were in on the robbery. Who's going to believe *your* story? I mean, come on – your sister is one of the crazies. They'll probably think you're the ringleader and you set up the whole scam."

Skip flipped his cigarette butt out the window. "Leon's house is about six blocks from here. Fasten your seatbelt, we're on our way."

Leon lived in a dingy Airstream trailer sitting up on concrete blocks. The tiny yard was overgrown and the gravel driveway was dotted with oil stains.

Skip parked the Toyota in the front and started to tell Chloe she needed to stay in the car. He didn't get to finish because she was already out of the door.

"You scare me sometimes," he said as he caught up with her. "The first time I met you, you seemed so frail and timid. And now look at you."

"I'm not Wonder Woman," Chloe said as she peered in through the trailer's dusty windows.

"I'm scared to death. But I can't stand by and let these jerks get away with this."

Skip hesitated, then said, "You're really a good friend, you know that?"

Chloe looked at her brother. "So are you." She surprised him with a quick hug. "I'm really glad you're here. I'd be even more afraid if you weren't."

"I'm glad, too," he replied. "Even if I do have an unbelievable headache, no job, and – if what you suspect is true – no real friends."

"You've got me," Chloe said.

"Yeah." He searched her eyes, no flippant humour in his gaze now. "I guess I have, haven't I?"

The trailer was almost empty, and there didn't appear to be any hidden cache of stolen goods.

"This is a dead end," Chloe muttered, turning to go back to the car.

"Where to now?" Skip asked.

"A phone booth." Chloe got in the Toyota, disregarding the curious stares of neighbours from surrounding trailers. "I need to find out where Robbie Proctor lives."

"That kid at the garden store? Why?" Skip put the car in gear and lurched down the road.

"Because I think he's the one who fixed my garden." Chloe told Skip about the secret gardener, and her belief that it was Robbie.

"That doesn't surprise me," Skip said, after hearing her tale. "I knew he liked you that first time we went to Helmsley's. But what's he got to do with this?"

"Robbie was at my garden last night round one-thirty. Maybe he passed the appliance store on his way home. If he did, he might have seen something."

Skip puffed out his cheeks. "OK. It's not a great lead, but it's all we've got."

Chloe found Robbie's address in the phone book. But when they arrived at his home, his mother told them Robbie wasn't there. She was a slim woman, and wearing headphones. An aerobics video was playing on the big-screen TV behind her.

"He's at his grandfather's farm," Mrs Proctor said. "Grandpa's sick and Robbie promised he'd help out till Grandpa feels better."

"When did he go?" Chloe asked.

Mrs Proctor smoothed her hair back as she thought. "It was late. Yesterday evening, shortly after dinner."

"But he couldn't have," Chloe blurted before she could stop. *He had to have been at my garden last night!*

"Oh, I'm certain of it," Mrs Proctor said.

"Robbie called from the farm before I went to bed."

"Thanks," Skip said, shaking Mrs Proctor's hand. "We'll talk to him when he gets back." He took Chloe's arm and led her away from the Proctor house.

"I couldn't be wrong about him," Chloe whispered when she got back in the car.

"Well, it doesn't really matter," Skip said. "Robbie's away and you can talk to him about it later. In the meantime, we need to figure out what to do about Earl and Leon. I believe you were dead right about them. They're our thieves. But how do we prove it?"

Chloe was too befuddled to think. *If Robbie wasn't in my garden last night, who was? I know I didn't imagine it. Was it someone else*?

Suddenly Chloe remembered the stories about the demons in the Clarksons' garden. Most of Hamilton seemed to believe the house was haunted. Maybe they were right!

Chapter Sixteen

Back home once more, Chloe went out to her garden to think. Weeding and tending the flower beds helped her focus.

"Nobody seems to know where Leon is," Skip called through the kitchen window. He'd been on the phone for the last half-hour trying to find Leon. "He never went back to the gas station and he's not answering at home." Skip slammed the phone down in disgust. "What did he think I would do – just curl up and let Quality Appliances fire me 'cause I fell asleep? That burns me up!"

Chloe kept pulling weeds mechanically. The world was doing an awfully good job of running over Chloe, her family and her friends. The urge to retreat into her room and never come out was furiously bubbling inside her. Before she could turn and run, a familiar voice barked at her from over the fence.

"I read about your friends in the paper!"

Startled, Chloe looked up and saw Colonel

Marquette in his trademark fishing hat, glaring at her over the fence.

"Didn't surprise me a bit," the colonel said. "I knew that centre was trouble from the minute they broke ground."

Unable to let his comments pass, Chloe collected all the anger she had inside and marched herself over to the fence. "My friends were set up."

"By whom?" the colonel scoffed.

"The Citizens' Alliance. You've been against the halfway house from the beginning."

"You're grasping at straws, young lady," the colonel scoffed. "I would never go against the laws governing this great country. I spent too many years fighting to preserve them."

"I know my friends are innocent," Chloe insisted. "What would anyone in that centre need with the things stolen from that appliance store?"

"You're assuming we're dealing with rational minds," the colonel reminded her. "I believe the thief – or thieves – stole those goods just for the thrill of stealing."

"Then where's the rest of the missing merchandise?" Chloe challenged. "That was a robbery, and someone is planning to make money from it."

"Maybe the lunatic has it squirrelled away

somewhere else," the colonel said. "Like a pack rat. What it might be worth could be of no consequence to him at all."

"You're right about the thief not having a rational mind," Chloe said. "Anyone who tries to hurt a place that helps people has got to be off their rocker."

"Young lady, if you are trying to implicate the Citizens' Alliance in this scandal," the colonel blustered, "you'd better watch your step. That's libel."

The thought suddenly occurred to her. *Maybe the Citizens' Alliance hired Leon and Earl to help them frame the centre.* It made sense in a weird way, but Chloe knew it'd be tough to prove.

"As far as I'm concerned, you and Mrs Helmsley are the prime suspects in this case. You know you don't have a legal leg to stand on to stop us – so you're resorting to dirty tricks to get your way. Well, I am going to work very hard to make sure justice is served and you are arrested."

"You can't go making wild accusations against people like that," the colonel said.

"Can't I? You seem to have no trouble doing it."

"That's where you're wrong," Marquette

replied. "If you ask me, I'd say the thief is that scar-faced boy the police suspect. I'm surprised they haven't arrested him."

"Eric?" Chloe was genuinely puzzled. "He would never hurt a soul. He rarely leaves the centre."

"Oh, is that so? Then why do I see him at your house so often? And always at night."

Chloe was stunned. Eric had only been to her house once.

"Oh yes," the colonel said. "I've seen him several times. He generally stops in the field on the other side of your wall, then puts on a dark cloak, like he's dressing up for some costume ball. Then once he's in that weird get-up, he spends hours pottering round in your garden."

Eric? He's my secret gardener? Chloe remembered the whispering voice, so full of feelings and dreams. *But why didn't he tell me?*

Then she remembered the story about the handsome prince and the dwarfish servant who loved him. Mignonette. The poor woman who loved the prince and required nothing from him but friendship. *Is that the way Eric feels about her?*

It was very confusing.

"I saw him here the night of the robbery," the colonel said. "He left your place about five minutes before the sirens went off. Of course, I phoned the police the instant I made the connection."

Chloe's heart pounded in her chest. "Do you mean to say, Colonel, that Eric could have left my house, crossed the field, circled back the ten blocks to town and broken into the appliance store – in *five* minutes?"

The colonel frowned. "Well, now that you put it that way... I, uh, well, he could have robbed the place before he came to your house and—"

"I don't have another second of my life to waste listening to you," said Chloe, in absolute disgust. She turned her back on him and hurried back towards the house.

As she passed through her garden, Chloe saw plants that reminded her of Monticello. And she remembered Eric's whispered conviction that she would make her garden look as beautiful as Jefferson's.

I have to go to him. Eric has to know I believe in him.

When Chloe got out of Skip's car in front of the centre, two policemen were escorting Eric in handcuffs to a waiting patrol car. She started towards him.

Skip caught her and held her back despite the

way she struggled. "Not now. You'll only make things worse."

Realizing the wisdom in her brother's words, Chloe stopped fighting and just let him hold her. Dr Laird stood silently with the other patients at the centre door, her arms crossed, her face taut with anguish. No one said anything as the police hustled Eric into the back seat, then drove away. Eric never turned round.

"What happened?" Chloe asked, rushing up to the group the second Skip let her go. She had to avoid the ride-on lawn mower parked against the steps.

"The police got a warrant to search Eric's room," Dr Laird said in a tired voice. "When they went through his things, they found a key that fitted the back door to the appliance shop. They arrested him and are going to keep him in jail."

"He was framed," Chloe protested.

"I know that," Dr Laird snapped. She softened her tone immediately, and said, "But I can't prove it."

The rest of the group looked shattered, and more than a little fearful. Eric's arrest represented their worst nightmares about the world outside the protective walls of the centre.

I've got to find a way to prove Eric's

innocence, Chloe thought, *or we're all going to lose our minds.*

As she thought, her eyes wandered idly across the yard. Chloe noticed that the gardening tools were stacked along one side of the building. She walked over to get a better look. There were pruning shears, rakes, hoes, and coils of garden hose.

"Those don't belong there," she announced.

"God, you are obsessed." Skip shook his head. "Your friend has just been taken to the police station and all you can think about is gardening."

"That's not it," Chloe said, touching a rake handle. She had attracted the attention of Dr Laird and the rest of the group. "It's just that these tools are always, *always* in the shed." She looked round some more, and found still other pieces of equipment left out. The spreader and mulcher were by the patio. The edger and roto-tiller looked as if they'd been deliberately placed by the hedge.

"So someone's going to use them," Skip said, with a shrug.

Dr Laird wore a puzzled look. "What's going on, Chloe?"

Chloe quickly explained her theory about Leon and Earl committing the actual robbery.

"My point is," she finished, "if these things aren't in the shed – what is?"

Everyone looked in the direction of the shed.

"The rest of the stolen goods," Skip murmured.

"If you're right," Lea said, "can't we just call the police and tell them?"

"That won't get Eric off the hook," Skip said, taking a cigarette out of his pocket and lighting it. "They'll think he stashed them there."

Chloe's mind raced as ideas took shape. "We're going to have to hand the police absolute proof that Earl and Leon staged the robbery and framed Eric. And I think I know how to do it." She looked at the group. "But I'm going to need the help of everyone here. Including you, Doc." Her eyes glinted with mischief. "We're not exactly going to break any rules, but we're certainly going to bend a few."

As Chloe described what she had in mind, the faces of the others began to brighten. Before she'd gone very far, the others were adding their own touches to the plan. Then Dr Laird added the most bizarre twist of all, and it fitted perfectly.

Chloe knew they were operating under the tightest of deadlines. Being confined to jail was a horrible ordeal for the healthiest of people.

Every moment Eric spent in confinement would only add one more indelible scar to his tortured soul.

Chapter Seventeen

That evening Chloe placed the call at a little after nine o'clock, knowing from Skip's investigation that Leon would be home then. She didn't give him time to think.

"I know who you are," she said in a firm voice. "And I know it was you who robbed Quality Appliances, not the boy the police have in jail right now."

"Who is this?" Leon demanded. He sounded scared.

"Chloe Summerlin." She stood in the big conference room at the centre, looking out of the window over the darkening landscape. She was a little frightened but Katie had assured her that Cancers could muster great courage when they needed it. And she needed it now.

"Skip's kid sister." Leon sounded a little more relaxed.

"That's an accident of birth," Chloe said in a harsh voice. "He was stupid. Letting you and Earl drug him with that high octane coffee."

"I think I'm going to hang up," Leon said. "You're a loony. Who's going to believe a word you say?"

"Then I guess you won't mind if I call the police and suggest they talk to you."

"I'll take my chances."

"Fine, but while you're taking your chances, let me remind you that you're taking a bigger chance by leaving the rest of those stolen goods in the gardening shed."

Leon's breathing sounded ragged over the phone. "What do you want?"

Now comes the part I really have to sell him on. "Money. I want money. To leave my brother, this loony bin, and this stupid hick town."

"Oh. You're trying to blackmail me."

"That's right. For a mere thousand dollars—" she hoped that didn't sound like too much or too little "—you get to keep the goods, and I'll keep my mouth shut."

"And if I don't pay?" Leon asked.

"Then I call the police and ask them to take a look at what Earl's got hidden in the gardening shed at the centre." Chloe paused to let the implication sink in. "Do you think Earl will take the blame alone?"

"For a loony, you think you're pretty smart," Leon said angrily. "I can see why Skip doesn't like you."

"Do we have a deal?"

"I don't have a choice. How do you want to do this?"

"Be at the centre at eleven o'clock with the money," Chloe instructed. "The big conference room. Earl knows the one. Don't be late."

She hung up, and found she was trembling like a leaf. Dr Laird put her arm round Chloe's shoulder.

"That was great, Chloe. Do you think you're going to be able to handle this?"

Chloe nodded. "I have to. If Leon doesn't see me when he gets here, this won't work at all."

"We could turn the stolen property over to the police," Dr Laird said, "and let them sort it out on their own."

"No! Eric can't stay in the jail another minute!" Chloe was surprised at the depth of feeling she had for him. "If this works, the police will set him free tonight." *If this works.* Chloe swallowed hard and tried not to think of the million things that could go wrong.

"They're here," Skip called from the window. He was dressed all in black, including a black cap that could be pulled over his face.

The conference room was dark now. Chloe paced beside the long table, rehearsing everything she was going to say. She took a deep breath, but the cold knot of fear in her stomach wouldn't go away.

"I'll be right outside if you need me," Skip promised. He squeezed her shoulder as he walked by. "I think you've got a lot of guts, sis."

"Thanks." She sat on the edge of the table near the small desk lamp and turned it on. Everything was going to happen very fast now. She could feel her heart beating.

It was quiet in the centre. The lights-out curfew was in effect, and no one was usually in the conference area at night anyway. Footsteps sounded in the hall, light taps that told Chloe whoever was coming was trying very hard not to be heard.

Her knees quivered and she willed them to relax. *Just think of Eric, what he must be feeling. You can't let these two goons keep him in jail.*

Earl came through the door first. His keys jangled on his belt. "Hello, Chloe," he said. "Didn't figure you for this."

"I guess we were both surprised," Chloe said evenly.

Leon followed Earl into the room, pulling the door shut behind him. He was dressed in a black

T-shirt and dark jeans. A short crowbar was in his hand. The desk lamp threw a soft incandescence on to it.

"It's too dark in here," Earl grumbled, starting for the light switches.

"Leave them off," Leon said, knocking his hand away. He looked hard at Chloe. "You ready to deal, girl?"

"Have you got the money?" Chloe asked.

Leon moved forward. Over his shoulder, Earl's face looked pasty and slack. "Sure. I got the money. But how can I be sure you won't turn me in anyway?" He was less than three metres away and closing slowly.

"You're going to have to trust me."

"What if I don't?" Leon was barely two metres away.

Chloe didn't make a reply. *Timing. Everything relied on timing.*

Leon was tense and jumpy.

"What if I decided to just cave in your head tonight?" Leon asked. "I wouldn't have to worry at all."

"Leon," Earl said.

"Shut up, Earl. You're partly to blame for this."

Leon was close enough for Chloe to smell corn chips on his breath. It was time to play her trump card.

"Mrs Clarkson told me she wouldn't let you hurt me."

Leon froze and looked confused. "What are you talking about? That old bat's dead and gone."

Chloe smiled agreeably. "She's dead, all right, but she's not gone. I found her in the garden behind the house. You were right. She's been there all along."

Leon licked his lips nervously. "You're crazy."

"That's only an opinion." She looked at him. "Don't you believe in ghosts? You're the one who told me that house was haunted. You said you'd been by there and seen things moving round in the garden at night."

"I was just a kid," Leon said. "Kids see things all the time that aren't there."

"Pay me," Chloe said, extending her hand, "or I'm calling the police tonight."

"I'm not going to pay you anything," Leon snarled. "If you're found dead in here, they'll just blame one of the loonies." He came forward again.

"Is that what you want, Earl?" Chloe asked as she backed away from Leon. "Do you want to be an accomplice to murder?"

"Hey, Leon, this isn't necessary," Earl said. "Just pay her the money and let's get out of here."

"We can't trust her. Only one way to shut her mouth permanently." Leon raised the crowbar.

"Mrs Clarkson!" Chloe screeched, dashing to the other side of the table. "Help me!" She pushed the table into Leon, slowing him down.

The desk lamp exploded in a brilliant flash of white. Leon ducked away, recoiling from the sudden glare. Then the room was black.

Even though she'd been prepared for it, Chloe's vision was still patchy. She wondered if Earl and Leon could see at all.

But there was no way to miss the unearthly apparition that stepped out from the wall at the front of the room. In the dark, the woman could only be seen as short and thick. Her dress swished round her, and her hair stuck out in all directions. A musty scent filled the air, and it smelled like the fresh-turned dirt on a grave.

"Leave her alone, Leon Mahaffey," an old crone's voice said. The figure moved steadily towards Leon.

Holding the crowbar in front of him, Leon backed across the room. "Get away from me before I hurt you!" He swung the crowbar in warning.

"I told you, Leon," Chloe said. "Mrs Clarkson told me she wouldn't let you hurt me."

Leon stumbled to the door and yanked on the knob. It didn't budge. "It's locked!" he yelled in horror. "Earl, we can't get out!"

Earl, who was cowering on the far side of the room, didn't respond.

Without the desk lamp, the room was filled with inky shadows that seemed to billow and move eerily. Chloe had to make her way round by touch and memory. Only the faces of the men and the apparition were visible to any degree.

"You saw the way Leon was going to hurt me," Chloe told Earl. "Do you really think he was going to trust you to keep your mouth shut too?"

"His soul is mine," the apparition said in its cold voice. "Confess your sins, Leon Mahaffey."

"Stay away from me!" With a growl of rage, Leon threw himself at the ghost. All that could be seen was his face and the dulled gleam of the crowbar as he raised it to swing.

The apparition threw her hand out in his direction. "No!" A split second later, Leon reversed direction and fell heavily to the ground. A black mist engulfed his face and he vanished. His scream was cut short.

"Leon?" Earl gaped at the black spot where

his cousin had been moments before. "Where are you?"

The apparition turned its attention to Earl, walking slowly towards him. "Do you believe in ghosts?" it demanded in the cold, thin voice.

"Yes," Earl said in a ragged whisper.

"Do you truly believe?"

"Yes." His answer was louder.

Incredibly, the apparition reached up and yanked at its hair. Its skin came off, leaving the gory red outlines of the skull beneath. The jaws worked up and down as the spectre screeched, "Then tell me the truth about the robbery!"

"We did it!" Earl shouted through broken sobs. "Me and Leon, we drugged Chloe's brother, then broke into the appliance store. After we stole the stuff, we stashed it in the shed, and put some of it in the centre to point the blame at the patients. Once we found out Eric Irons was suspected of doing the robbery, Leon had me put a key in his room. Oh god, please don't kill me."

There was a rustle of fabric on the floor and Leon's voice shouted, "Earl, you big idiot, shut your mouth."

The skull grinned and moved away.

"Thanks," Chloe said, looking at Earl. "I think that's all we need. How about it, Chief?"

"Yes," a bass voice said. "That's enough for me."

"Somebody get the lights," Chloe ordered. An instant later, the track lighting overhead came on, revealing Skip on the floor holding Leon. Dr Laird stood in front of Earl, the black-light paint still smearing her features in the blurred outlines of a skull. She held a rubber mask with fright wig in one hand.

Three uniformed policemen came from behind the one-way mirror at the opposite end of the conference room and took charge of the two stunned thieves. A tall, barrel-chested man in a trench coat and business suit came in as well, holding up a black plastic video cassette in one hand.

"Got it all on video," Police Chief Tolliver declared in his deep voice.

"Terrific," Dr Laird said, stripping the rubber skincap from her head and letting her hair loose. "I don't think I've ever looked better."

"I'd put you up for an Academy Award if I could," Chief Tolliver said. "I had to remind myself a couple of times that it was all an act."

"I really don't believe you," the doctor replied with a grin. "But I thank you for saying that."

"And as for you, young lady." The chief

turned to Chloe, nodding in amazement. "When you came to me this evening with this harebrained scheme, I figured we'd be better off recovering the stolen property tonight and do the questioning in the morning."

"There's no need for questions now, is there?" Chloe asked.

"No." The chief glanced at Leon and Earl, who were handcuffed and being led out of the door while listening to their rights.

"So Eric can be released tonight?" Chloe asked.

"As soon as I make a phone call," Chief Tolliver replied. He looked at her. "You know, that boy Eric should consider himself damn lucky to have a friend like you."

"Thanks." Chloe felt herself blushing.

Skip threw his arm round her. "That's my sis," he said proudly.

CHAPTER EIGHTEEN

Later that evening Chloe stood in the shadows by the Hamilton police station and watched Skip and Eric come out of the building. She'd persuaded Dr Laird to let Skip and her bring Eric back to the centre by themselves. The doctor had readily agreed, saying that Eric probably needed some one-on-one time before getting mobbed by the other patients.

The street in front of the police station was totally deserted. A few blocks down, two firemen were sitting on benches in front of the firehouse, talking. The shadows were drawn tall and deep, not bothered at all by the light breeze that flitted through the town.

"You wait right here," Skip told Eric, "and I'll bring the car round."

Eric nodded. He was in his usual denim shirt and jeans, the familiar Australian stockman's hat in one hand. With his shoulders bowed, he looked small and crumpled.

"Eric, it's me," Chloe called from the

shadows.

He started to turn to face her when she said, "Please don't turn round."

"Why?" He sounded uneasy but did as she asked.

"Because I want you to know how it feels to talk to someone and not be able to see their face."

"What?" He started to turn again.

"Don't turn," she ordered.

"Is this a joke? Because I'm really not in the mood for it."

"It's no joke," Chloe said. "When I found out you were my secret gardener, I was a little upset – and hurt – that you didn't have the courage to face me, since I've always been your friend. Then I realized that maybe you were more comfortable talking about things when you thought I couldn't see you."

"I could tell you that I don't know what you're talking about," Eric whispered.

"Don't try," Chloe advised. "My neighbour saw you in my garden. That's why you were arrested by the police, because he recognized you."

Skip pulled the Toyota round the building and left the lights off. Chloe motioned him to stay in the car.

Eric was silent for a while. "Are you mad at me?"

"How could I be," Chloe answered. "You saved me, Eric. I'd given up. My garden seemed to represent my life – just an empty weedpit."

"I just read a few books," Eric said. "Made the soil healthy. It wasn't much."

"It was more than you could ever imagine." Chloe stepped out of the shadows and walked in front of him.

He put his hat on self-consciously, turning his face so that his good side was towards her. "You were being kind of hard on yourself," he mumbled.

"I don't exactly have a monopoly on that, do I?"

He looked like he was about to disagree but Chloe met his gaze directly. "Probably not," he admitted.

"Life outside the centre is filled with surprises," she told him. "I know there will always be bad things that happen in the world. But I also know that we can survive anything – if we have friends who believe in us."

Eric smiled at Chloe, a shy, crooked smile.

She took his hand. "Would you come and work with me in my garden this summer?"

"I'd like that," Eric whispered. "A lot."

Chloe stood on tiptoe and gently pressed her lips to his.

Eric kissed back, timidly at first, then with more confidence. When they pulled back, his eyes were twinkling.

Skip was grinning from ear to ear when they got in the car.

"You know, sis," he said, as the car pulled away from the kerb. "I've been thinking. That house is awfully big for just the two of us. I thought maybe we could talk to the Doc to see about getting the centre to buy it as their halfway house. Maybe I could help in group counselling. Well, maybe not... But I could be the, uh, chaperon. Or chauffeur. Whatever. And it would be nice to have a family in there. One big, happy family." Skip looked at Chloe in the rearview mirror. "What do you think?"

Chloe raised an eyebrow. "I'd say you're out of your mind." She grinned at Eric happily. "But since we're all a bunch of lunatics anyway – let's go for it!"

*ARIES*TAURUS*GEMINI*CANCER*LEO*VIRGO*LIBRA*
*SCORPIO*SAGITTARIUS*CAPRICORN*AQUARIUS*PISCES*

Twelve signs of the Zodiac. Twelve novels, each one embracing the characteristics of a zodiac sign. Pushed to the extreme, these characteristics lead down twisting paths into tales of mystery, horror, romance and fantasy.

Whatever your sun sign, you will want to read Zodiac, the series written in the stars.

ARIES	SECRET IDENTITY
TAURUS	BLACK OUT
GEMINI	MIRROR IMAGE
CANCER	DARK SHADOWS
LEO	STAGE FRIGHT
VIRGO	DESPERATELY YOURS
LIBRA	FROZEN IN TIME
SCORPIO	DEATH GRIP
SAGITTARIUS	STRANGE DESTINY
CAPRICORN	DON'T LOOK BACK
AQUARIUS	SECOND SIGHT
PISCES	SIXTH SENSE

SERIES CREATED BY JAHNNA N. MALCOLM

PISCES:
A DREAMER, KNOWS SECRETS
SIXTH SENSE

*P*hoebe is a loner. She can sense when something's wrong, but people distrust her and are afraid of her premonitions. When Mark Chenier disappears, images grow in Phoebe's mind – she knows where Mark is, but no one, except her Cajun grandmother, believes her. Can she prove that she is right and that her 'dreams' really tell the truth?

SCORPIO:
PASSIONATE, FORCEFUL
DEATH GRIP

*S*abrina loves with a fierce intensity - even those who have died. First her mother drowns, and then Matt... Can *his* death really have been an accident or was it cold-blooded murder? Sabrina is determined to discover the truth - even if it means enlisting the help of a spirit from beyond the grave.

TAURUS:
PATIENT, PRACTICAL
BLACK OUT

*T*ess can't remember much. Except that the Halloween party went wrong. There was a fire and people were trapped. But it wasn't an accident. Tess knows who the murderer is – if only she could remember… Her patience is put to the test in a deadly waiting game.

VIRGO:
PERFECTIONIST, ORDERLY
DESPERATELY YOURS

*V*irginia is always in control, so when disturbing letters arrive at her school newspaper office from someone signed Desperate, it is Virginia who deals with them. But when a friend dies, a photograph is maliciously destroyed and the letters from Desperate become more threatening… Virginia's orderly world is tested to the limit.